King Kong and Other Poets

D0962391

ALSO BY ROBERT BURCH

D.J.'s Worst Enemy

Queenie Peavy

Hut School and the
Wartime Home-Front Heroes

Two That Were Tough

Wilkin's Ghost

Ida Early Comes Over the Mountain

Christmas with Ida Early

KING KONG
and Other Poets

BY ROBERT BURCH

Viking Kestrel

For Daniel Scovill
and
Hope Scovill

VIKING KESTREL
Viking Penguin, Inc., 40 West 23rd Street, New York, New York 10010, U.S.A.
Penguin Books Ltd, Harmondsworth, Middlesex, England
Penguin Books Australia Ltd, Ringwood, Victoria, Australia
Penguin Books Canada Limited, 2801 John Street, Markham, Ontario, Canada L3R 1B4
Penguin Books (N.Z.) Ltd, 182–190 Wairau Road, Auckland 10, New Zealand

Copyright © Robert Burch, 1986
All rights reserved
First published in 1986 by Viking Penguin Inc.
Published simultaneously in Canada
Printed in U.S.A. by The Book Press, Brattleboro, Vermont
Set in Garamond #3
1   2   3   4   5   90   89   88   87   86

Library of Congress Cataloging in Publication Data
Burch, Robert.   King Kong and other poets.
Summary: A shy new girl makes a place for herself
in her sixth-grade class by writing poems.
[1. Poets—Fiction.   2. Bashfulness—Fiction.   3. Schools—Fiction.]   I. Title.
PZ7.B91585Ki   1986   [Fic]   86-5512   ISBN 0-670-80927-6

Without limiting the rights under copyright reserved above, no part of this
publication may be reproduced, stored in or introduced into a retrieval system,
or transmitted, in any form or by any means (electronic, mechanical, photocopying,
recording or otherwise), without the prior written permission of both the
copyright owner and the above publisher of this book.

King Kong and Other Poets

Contest

What was the new girl's name? If Andy could have thought of it, he'd have called on her. Nobody had called on her; maybe none of the other sixth-graders could remember her name either.

Mrs. Todd was having the students review their work of the first six weeks by asking each other questions. Tomorrow there'd be tests.

When Andy finished his turn asking questions, he sat down and looked out the window. Now he could watch the airstrip across the highway. The blue-and-white Cessna Skyhawk, the plane he and his classmates called the Jaybird, was coming in for a landing now. It always bounced twice.

Andy planned to be a pilot someday; he'd bet he could put the Jaybird on the ground without bouncing even once.

Mrs. Todd asked the questions now: "What oceans surround Asia? Andy, can you tell us?"

He did not hear her. He'd just sat down; he was sure she wouldn't call on him so soon.

"Then could you tell us *how many* oceans surround Asia?" When he still did not answer, she said loudly, "Andy, how many?"

"Oh," said Andy, shaking his head as if he'd been in a daze. "That's the fifth one this morning."

His classmates laughed, and Mrs. Todd smiled. "We're talking about continents and oceans, not planes." The bell rang, and she added: "Maybe someone will tell you at recess what the question was."

The class started outside, and the new girl, back of Andy in line, said, "Sometimes I do the same thing."

He looked back to see who was with her and was surprised that she was talking to him. "Do what?" he asked.

"Lose myself in something I'm thinking about till it seems more real than what's real."

"It *was* real," said Andy. "I was watching the Jaybird come in for a landing."

"There's nothing wrong in daydreaming," said the new girl, just as they got outside.

Andy looked at her. *"Marilyn,"* he said. "That's your name: *Marilyn.*"

"Yes, I know," she said softly, walking out across the

playground. Andy supposed she was going out to talk to some of the girls, but when the bell rang to go back inside, he noticed that she was sitting by herself on a rock near the edge of the schoolyard.

Andy wondered if anyone else had remembered her name. She'd been introduced to the class last Monday, exactly a week ago, the day she'd arrived. School had been under way over a month by then, and the others already had their own friends—and enemies too, perhaps.

It was partly her fault, thought Andy, that nobody knew her. She hadn't made any effort to be friendly. Till the conversation at the beginning of recess, she hadn't said a word to him. But then, he hadn't said a word to her either. And, too, although she may not have appeared friendly, he had to admit that she hadn't done anything to bother anyone.

When the students had settled back into their places, Mrs. Todd said, "We'll continue with our review. Marilyn, would you like to ask the questions?"

"No, ma'am," said Marilyn. "I don't believe I would."

The children laughed. Nobody ever turned down a chance to be the teacher. You could keep the book open if you liked and didn't have to worry about not knowing answers. And besides, when Mrs. Todd said, "Wouldn't you like to do something?" it really meant, "Do it!"

Marilyn hadn't answered in a smart-alecky way. In her soft voice, she'd merely declined the opportunity to be the teacher for a few moments.

"Why not?" asked Mrs. Todd. "Why wouldn't you like to ask the questions?"

"It's just that I don't know everybody's name."

"In that case, *now* would be a very good time to start learning them. Come to the front of the room, and bring your book with you."

Marilyn stepped to the front of the class. She's mousy-looking, thought Andy. No wonder nobody's paid any attention to her. Her hair was stringy and not quite brown, yet not really blond. *Dishwatery,* he'd heard such coloring described. Her clothes, although they looked new, were also drab; they might be called dishwatery, too. Her eyes were her best feature. They were a clear, cool green; the color reminded Andy of limeade. Otherwise, Marilyn's looks were very ordinary. She was about average height, he'd say, but so skinny—and serious. He wondered if she'd ever smiled.

It turned out that Marilyn knew the names of quite a few of her classmates, after all, including Andy's. He'd have been just as glad if she had forgotten his. She asked him, "What's the greatest river in Africa?" and he didn't know. He wished someone else would miss it, too—that always made him feel better—but Marilyn called on Sue Brady next, and Sue, as always, knew everything. "The greatest river in Africa is the Nile," she said. "And life in Egypt centers around it." Andy would be willing to bet that was exactly what the book had said about the Nile.

Soon Andy became absorbed in another plane that was

landing at the airstrip across the highway. It was the private airport for the ritzy resort, Garden Hills, in the distance. He was happy to see that the new plane was the splendid Learjet from California that the class had dubbed the Yellow Daisy. This was the first time it had been here since school started. It had come often last year and was everyone's favorite.

A sleek black limousine rolled onto the field and parked near the plane, blocking Andy's view of the jet's door. Until last year, limousines were a rarity in Flag City, Georgia, but now they were seen frequently. Some of the people flying into Garden Hills were met by them. Sometimes a limousine parked near the runway before the plane arrived. Andy always kept a keen eye out then because chances were good that no ordinary plane was about to land.

There were rumors that the Yellow Daisy belonged to a big man in movies, a Hollywood producer, who came here every few months. It was said that he could meet business associates from the Southeast for golfing and tennis at Garden Hills.

Nobody in Flag City—at least, nobody Andy knew—ever went to Garden Hills. The two golf courses there were among the best in the United States, and membership in the club was very expensive. Although few townspeople could be a part of Garden Hills, it made everyone feel proud that such a grand resort was there. It was pleasant just to ride past it and see the handsome buildings—the big clubhouse itself, the tree-shaded guest cottages, and the big houses of the permanent residents. A pond here and there added to the beauty of the carefully kept grounds.

"Just look at it," Louisa had said this morning on the bus coming to school. She and Karen were on the seat in front of Andy and Blake. They'd come the same route many times, but the view today did seem special. There'd been a heavy dew, and the morning sun shining on the damp grass of the golf courses made the rolling hills look as if they'd been covered in green velvet.

"Can you imagine living in such a gorgeous place?" asked Karen.

Blake said, "*Imagine it* is all you can do!"

A single white duck bobbed about on a small pond near the fence.

"I don't care," said Louisa. "It's all so beautiful. It looks like something out of a book."

"What kind of book?" asked Blake, teasing her.

"A fairy tale," said Louisa, "where everything's perfect."

Early in the afternoon, an announcement came over the school intercom that it was time for assembly. The three sixth-grade rooms joined the other classes in the auditorium.

After everyone was seated, Mr. Gray, the principal of Stokes Elementary, made announcements. Then he introduced Miss Hayworth, a young reporter with the *Flag City Herald,* the town's daily newspaper.

Miss Hayworth was there to talk about a poetry-writing contest that the *Herald* was sponsoring. "Students from all five of the city's elementary schools are invited to participate," she said. "Each school will then submit winning entries for judging." She went on to tell about the deadline, two weeks away, and how all poems should be written neatly so that the judges would have no difficulty in reading them. "Of course, a prize will be given to the winner," she concluded. "Are there any questions?"

Jason raised his hand. "What's the prize?"

"A book of poetry," said Miss Hayworth. When a few of the students groaned, she appeared embarrassed. "It's a nice big book of poetry. A collection of poems, in fact. An anthology." Nobody else asked a question about the poetry contest.

Back in their room after assembly, some of the sixth-graders agreed that the prize wasn't worth making any real effort to win.

"Why couldn't it be a tape of Dumbo Brink?" asked Karen. Dumbo Brink was her favorite recording star. "Or some really neat stickers?"

"Or a model plane?" suggested Andy.

"Or an electric mirror?" said Patsy.

"An *electric mirror!*" shouted Jason.

"You know, a makeup mirror with lights around it." She fluffed up her hair in back. "That's what I'd call a good prize."

Marilyn, for the first time since she joined the class,

spoke up enthusiastically: "I think a book of poetry is a wonderful prize."

"Aw, go away!" said Jason, flipping out his hand as if he were shooing off something.

"Now, now!" said Mrs. Todd. "And I must say I'm pleased that at least one of my students is interested in poetry. For the rest of you, I might add this: there's more to winning a poetry-writing contest than the actual prize, which I agree with Marilyn is very nice indeed."

"What else is there?" asked Blake.

"Well, for one thing, if the student body hadn't been so uninterested after the nice young reporter mentioned the prize, she'd have gone on to tell you that the winning poem will be published in the paper. And most likely there'll be an article about the student who wrote it."

"Instant fame!" said Jason. "Maybe I'll write a poem after all."

Patsy asked, "Do you think they might put a picture of the person in the paper?"

"Perhaps."

"In that case, I think I'll write one, too."

"We'll get back to our review now," said Mrs. Todd. "But after we finish our tests tomorrow, I'll give over some class time to poetry-writing. I won't grade you. But who knows, it might be fun."

Andy thought about it later in the afternoon, while he stood at the busy intersection outside the public library. He'd ridden downtown with his mother. She had dropped him off, while she and Dru, his sister, went to the supermarket. In the library, he'd been disappointed that none of the new issues of aviation magazines had come in, and after a brief chat with Mrs. Noles, the librarian, he had decided to walk ahead to the supermarket instead of waiting to be picked up.

It always seemed to Andy that the light stayed red forever, and it was while waiting for it to change that he'd started thinking about the poetry-writing contest. Maybe he'd try to write a good poem; he wondered if he'd have a chance of winning. His parents had given him a poetry anthology last Christmas, but it might be nice to have another one. He thought about the new girl and how she'd brightened at the mention of the prize. Anyone would have thought a collection of poetry was the greatest thing in the world.

The light changed, and he started across the street. A van in one of the lanes across from him stalled, and it sounded as if drivers everywhere began blowing their horns. Andy looked back at the long line of cars. One of them was a limousine. He wondered if it could be the same one he'd seen at the airstrip earlier. Probably not.

As he walked down the block, the noise was deafening. Maybe he could write a poem about how much more pleasant it would be to fly around in the sky than have to put up with late-afternoon traffic snarls on the ground. He tried to think how to begin it, but no ideas came to him.

Ahead he saw his mother coming out of the supermarket. It looked as if she were being followed across the parking lot by a lone shopping cart. He knew that the cart was being pushed by five-year-old Dru, who was not tall enough to be seen over it. Dru always insisted on doing the pushing.

Car horns had eased up by now, and traffic, at last, was flowing smoothly. Andy looked up just as the limousine went past. Although he saw it across three lanes of automobiles, he could tell that two men were sitting on the back seat, talking, while a girl in the jump seat on the opposite side looked out a window. From his quick glimpse, she looked like the new girl from school, but Andy knew it wasn't. Nobody he knew would be riding in a limousine. His mind was playing tricks on him. He'd been thinking about her, and then, all of a sudden, there she was! Funny, he thought, if his imagination was so good, why couldn't he think of how to begin his poem?

King Kong
and Other Poets

"What can we write about?" asked Dave. The poetry-writing session was just getting under way.

"Well," said Mrs. Todd. "You could write about something exciting that you've done."

"I've never done anything exciting."

"Oh, come, come!" said Mrs. Todd, impatiently. "Certainly you have. But if you'd like, you could write about something quiet—a view you've admired—peach orchards in bloom or a nice sunset. Or you could write about your pets. Use your imagination."

Lena said, "Nothing's ever happened to me that's worth writing about."

"Everyone has something to write about. Just give it some thought. Now get busy!"

A few moments later Rip asked, "How do you like this:

> We started out,
>   but the car broke down,
> So me and the others
>   had to walk to town."

Mrs. Todd smiled. "I'd say it needs a bit of work. And let's try to write a poem, not just a short rhyme."

"What rhymes with pizza?" asked Cal.

"Nothing," said Jason. "Change it to *steak* and rhyme it with *cake.*"

"Or *shake*," suggested Andy.

"Change it to *custard* and rhyme it with *mustard*," said Tubby Williams.

"All right, let's not be silly," said Mrs. Todd, and everyone settled down to writing.

Toward the end of the period, Sue asked, "Do you want us to turn them in today?"

"No, you may want to work on them at home. Why not turn them in a week from today? And don't forget, you're to use a pseudonym instead of your own name. That was one of the things Miss Hayworth mentioned."

"What's a pseudonym?" asked Rip.

"It's a name other than your own. A fictitious or pen name."

"An alias, like on TV?" asked Patsy.

"Yes, that's right."

"How will anybody know then who really wrote the poems?" asked Andy.

"You'll put your pen name on the poem itself. Then write the pen name on an envelope—I have some that I'll give you. Then, inside the envelope, put a scrap of paper with your real name on it."

"I know what my pen name will be," said Rip. "Tarzan." He stood up and pounded his chest. "Me Tarzan!"

"That will defeat the purpose of the pen name if we know who it is. Therefore, Rip, you must select something else, or we'll all know that Tarzan is really Rip Larsen. It might be interesting if each one of you would keep your pen name a secret. Then when you're helping me select the best poems, you'll think about the poem itself instead of what you think of the person who wrote it. Would you agree to keep your pen names to yourselves?"

Everyone agreed to it, and Mrs. Todd said, "Fine! And now it's time for science."

That was the last time the poetry-writing contest was mentioned until the day the poems were turned in. "I'll read them this afternoon during English," said Mrs. Todd, "and we'll decide on the best ones. You can vote for your favorites."

At the beginning of English, Mrs. Todd flipped through the envelopes, smiling as she looked at the names on them. "We have poems by rock stars," she said, "sports figures, newscasters, and people from the past—Marco Polo, Abraham Lincoln, George Washington. Here's one by Rudolph, the Red-Nosed Reindeer. In fact, animals are well represented. Here's one by Garfield and one by Snoopy. And one by King Kong." Andy was pleased when his classmates laughed. King Kong was his pseudonym. He admitted to himself, however, that his pen name was better than his poem.

The first poem was called "My Cat and Her Kittens" and was by Chris Evert Lloyd. After she'd read it aloud, Mrs. Todd asked for comments.

"Who's Chris Evert Lloyd?" asked Matt.

"A tennis champion. But what did you think of the poem?"

"Maybe the next one will be better," said Matt, and evidently Mrs. Todd hoped so, too, because she took out another poem. "This one's by Alexander the Great, Military Conqueror and King of Macedonia. I don't know about the poem, but the pen name leads me to believe that somebody's been paying attention in social studies. Here's the way it goes:

Once I took a river ride
    With my brother and his bride
It was just before their wedding day
    Which is over now, and they're home to stay.

When they got back from their honeymoon
    They moved in with us and took over my room
If we go on the river for another ride
    I wish that I could drown the bride.

Andy knew that the poem was by Blake Knox. His brother had married recently, and Blake had been complaining that the newlyweds, instead of moving into a place of their own, were living with the family.

Mrs. Todd said, "Well, I'm sure that we all hope Alexander the Great, Military Conqueror and King of Macedonia, and his new sister-in-law will get on better in the future. But what do you think of the poem? Louisa, what did you think of it?"

"I thought it was cute," said Louisa. There weren't many things that Louisa didn't think were cute.

"Would someone else comment on it? Marilyn, how'd you like it?"

"I liked it," said Marilyn. "I wished it had gone on. The first two lines, 'Once I took a river ride / With my brother and his bride,' sounded so good that I'd have liked more of the same—except different."

"The same, but different!" said Jason. "Are you crazy?"

"No," said Marilyn, sounding much more serious about discussing a poem than anyone else had been. "I mean the next verse could have been, say, 'Then I took a highway trip . . . or a buggy ride . . . or went cross-country on a motorcycle . . . different things, but always at the end wishing something terrible had happened to the bride."

Mrs. Todd said, "Then it didn't bother you that the last line was rather drastic—even perverse?"

"Oh, no," said Marilyn. "The last line was best of all. And it *is* a poem. And if the newlyweds have taken over somebody's room, I'm for the one who's lost his own private space."

Andy thought: She's made a friend of Blake, that's for sure. Some of the girls in the class, however, did not share Marilyn's views of it. "Oh, that's awful!" said Sue, with a little shudder. "How could you like a poem like that?"

"My mama went to the wedding," said Lena. "And she said the bride was the prettiest thing she ever saw. How could you even stand to think of her drowning?"

Marilyn said, "I'm not even sure but what I'd have enjoyed it more if the poet had used something besides 'wishing.' "

"Such as what?" asked Mrs. Todd.

"Well, he could have . . . Let me think. Oh, I know, he could have ended it with, 'When we go on the river for another ride, / My mind's made up: I'll drown the bride.' That's better than just wishing it."

Some of the girls gasped, and even Mrs. Todd looked surprised.

Blake said, "Yeah, you're right. That would be better."

Dave said, "No, it wouldn't. You couldn't say that because it's not true."

"But everything's happened to me," insisted Blake. "Except drowning my new sister-in-law."

"Now, now!" said Mrs. Todd. "The pen names aren't effective if everyone knows the real author. But I suppose we'd all guessed this one was yours." She put it to the back of the sheaf of papers. "I'll read another one. Now try to think as Marilyn did about what you like, and how you really feel on hearing the poem. And make suggestions for ways to improve it if you have ideas. Very good, Marilyn!"

Andy was glad there was something that Marilyn could do. In math this morning, she'd missed almost all the problems, even the easy ones.

The next poem was by Princess Di and was about going to a family reunion and how everybody had told her how pretty she was. They'd said that she was just about the nicest-looking girl they'd ever seen. She hoped she would grow up to be even more beautiful.

Andy knew it was by Patsy Dalton. Patsy was forever telling about compliments people paid her on her looks. At the end of the poem, Mrs. Todd asked the class, "Well, what do you think?"

Rip said, "It made me want to throw up."

"Now, Rip!" scolded Mrs. Todd.

"But you said for us to say how we really felt on hearing it, and that's how I really felt."

Louisa, of course, thought the poem was cute, and Jason said, "So cute it stinks!"

Mrs. Todd asked Marilyn what she'd thought of it, and Marilyn said, "I didn't think it was very good." Patsy glared at her. If anybody had had any doubts about who Princess Di really was, they'd know now.

Blake said, "I'd rather be smart than good-looking."

"Too bad you're not either," said Jason.

"Now, hush, boys. You didn't give Marilyn a chance to finish her criticism. Go ahead, Marilyn."

"Well, I agree with Blake," said Marilyn. "I'd rather be told that I could figure out how to work tomorrow's math assignment than be told how I look." Patsy smirked as Marilyn continued: "But if I came across a poem like it in a book, probably for a little while I'd imagine myself pretty and being complimented by relatives. Maybe that would be nice."

Andy thought to himself that he could offer to help Marilyn with her math homework. It was the one subject that he really liked. He'd seen her at the library downtown after school several times; maybe he'd go again this afternoon.

There were other poems, most of them not very good—including Andy's, or King Kong's, "Traffic Jam." The only favorable comment on it came from Mrs. Todd. She said the idea was good. Another poem was called "My Dog Plays Fetch with Me" and went on and on about throwing a stick across the yard and how the dog would run after it and bring it back. Sometimes the dog would drop the stick at the boy's feet, and sometimes the boy would have to coax the dog into dropping it.

Andy concentrated on an Aero Commander that was landing at the Garden Hills airport. It was the first time he'd seen one of them, but he recognized it from a model that Cal had made. He watched two men and two women get off the plane, then he paid attention to the poems again.

"What did you think?" asked Mrs. Todd.

She looked at Andy, and he was relieved when Louisa said, "It was cute." When nobody else had a comment, Mrs. Todd picked up the next poem. "This one is called 'My Pets' and is by Ruby Duff."

"Who's Ruby Duff?" asked Sue.

"I don't know," said Mrs. Todd.

"Make 'em take it back," said Dave. "You said our pen names were supposed to be real names."

"No, I said that the pen names *could* be the names of real people—but not that they *had* to be. Now see what you think of the poem:

> My pet duck's name is Rinny-tin-tin,
> > My tomcat's name is Rover.
> They chase each other around the pond
> > And through a patch of clover.
>
> My pet squirrel's name is Fido,
> > My rabbit's name is Spot,
> They run away when Rover's near,
> > Because he acts friendly when he's not.
>
> My chipmunk, Benji, learned that lesson,
> > When he decided to be brave.
> The cat pretended to be playing,
> > Now my Benji's in his grave.
>
> I have a parrot called Big Red,
> > A canary who's Ol' Yellow,

And a guppy, Savage Sam,
    Who is a splendid fellow.

My favorite pet's an alligator,
    She's two feet long and sassy.
I'm training her to bite someone,
    I say, "Go get him, Lassie!"

I love the alligator,
    The rabbit, squirrel, and duck.
In fact, I truly know
    That I've had lots of luck.

I even love the tomcat,
    I love the birds and guppy.
I know that I should not complain,
    And yet . . . I've never had a puppy.

"Say!" said Jason. "That was okay."

"Be critical now and tell us what you did and didn't like about it."

"I wonder who wrote it," said Karen, looking around the room.

Andy believed it was by Marilyn, hard as it was to see how someone so mousy-looking and serious could write something that had made him laugh. But he knew that none of his other classmates had such a variety of pets. He was surprised when Mrs. Todd called on Marilyn for her opinion of the poem; maybe she hadn't written it.

"I didn't like the title at all," said Marilyn. " 'My Pets' sounds dull."

Patsy sat forward in her seat. "I like it!" she said, angrily. "I like the title." Andy knew that Patsy just wanted to disagree with Marilyn because Marilyn hadn't agreed with her that being pretty matters a whole lot. He noticed a little smile cross Marilyn's lips.

"Louisa, what did you think of it?" asked Mrs. Todd.

Jason and Blake said at the same time: "She thought it was *cute!*"

Louisa looked back at the boys and giggled. "No, I thought it was better than cute. I wish I'd written it, and I wish I had all those pets. I vote for it to be the winner."

the Winner *Is* . . .

Ruby Duff's poem was the pick of everyone in the class. "All right," said Mrs. Todd, "we'll submit it as one of our favorites. Now help me select two others. Mr. Gray asked that each room turn in three."

There was little agreement on the other two choices. Jason said he didn't think anything else was good enough to submit. Louisa, on the other hand, thought everything was. When Mrs. Todd called for a show of hands, the poems receiving the most votes were "Birthday Party," by Christopher Columbus, and one that Andy had especially liked—"The Rained-Out Picnic," by Minnie Mouse. It told about a picnic held on the grounds of Garden Hills just before the resort had been completed, when anyone could visit the lakes and ponds there.

Andy and his family had ridden through the grounds practically every Sunday afternoon when the resort was nearing completion. He had never seen so much heavy equipment in his life. One Sunday there'd be a dam finished and water beginning to accumulate for a lake where once there'd been a field of soybeans. Or the airstrip was being paved or new roads cut, or the clubhouse and residences were taking shape. The two golf courses had been laid out first, then suddenly they were green and manicured. Each week his father would marvel at all that had been done since the last time he'd seen it. He always said at the end of the outing, "It'll sure take money to pay for it," as if there were a chance that it would be paid for with anything else. Then suddenly gates were closed and locked or guarded; signs reading FOR MEMBERS ONLY were put up; and the resort was in business. Andy's father had said that people with money had arrived and townsfolk—most of them, at any rate—could forget about enjoying the resort as if it were a public park. Their day was over.

In the poem, "The Rained-Out Picnic," the picnic was called off because of bad weather. By the time it had been rescheduled, the resort had opened, and outsiders were no longer welcome. Andy could sympathize. The Sunday his family had first found the gates locked, they had wanted to show off the place to his grandparents, who were visiting from North Carolina. If Andy had written a poem about it, he'd have used as the title "For Members Only."

"Now we'll find out who the poets really are," said Mrs. Todd, opening an envelope. "Minnie Mouse is none other than Sue Brady."

Andy was disappointed. She was so smart—and so smug about being smart—that he'd have never voted for "The Rained-Out Picnic" if he'd known it was hers. Still, he supposed that really was the way of pen names. You judged the poem rather than the writer.

"Congratulations, Sue," said Mrs. Todd, as she opened another envelope. "And our next winner is Christopher Columbus, better known as Matt Melton."

"Who's Ruby Duff?" asked Karen.

"Well, let me see if I can find the envelope with that name on it."

Louisa giggled. "This is like the Academy Awards." As if she were a presenter on a television awards program, she said, "The envelope, please!"

"Ah, here it is," said Mrs. Todd, opening the third envelope. "Ruby Duff, it turns out, is our newest class member, Marilyn Peck."

"Marilyn Peck?" said Patsy, turning to Marilyn. "You wrote that poem? But you said you didn't like the title."

Marilyn smiled. "I didn't," she said, "but I was glad that you did."

Sue Brady, a worried look on her face, asked Mrs. Todd, "When you turn in the poems, will you tell Mr. Gray how many votes each one got?"

"No, I'll just give him the three we've chosen. Someone else will do the judging for the school."

Sue looked relieved, and Patsy said, "I imagine Sue's poem will win." Everyone else was confident Marilyn's would be chosen. "Oh, yes," said Jason. " 'My Pets' is the best poem of all."

Emily looked at Marilyn. "It must be neat to have all those pets."

Karen said, "I figured you lived out in the country, but I didn't know you had so many pets. You've got a regular circus."

"A menagerie," corrected Mrs. Todd.

Other students said how much fun it must be to have so many pets. Blake said, "But I'm sorry you don't have a dog, too."

Andy noticed that Marilyn didn't say anything. Maybe nobody gave her a chance. She let her classmates do the talking; all she did was look pleased.

After school, Andy went to the town library. In the reading room, Mrs. Noles greeted him with, "The new issue of *Aviation Week* has come in. That's the good news. The bad news is that someone else has it." Pointing toward the door to the courtyard reading area, she added: "A man took it. But it's too chilly to sit out there long; I'd guess he'll bring it back soon."

Andy went out to the courtyard. Sometimes people took several magazines out there, and if the man happened not to be reading *Aviation,* maybe he could borrow it for a few moments.

The only person in the courtyard was a tall man, sitting

on a concrete bench. He wore khaki work clothes, and a cowboy hat was pushed back on his head. The magazine was on the bench beside him. Andy went nearer, but the man did not notice him. Perhaps he was asleep. Then Andy saw that the man's eyes were wide open and he was staring into space. The eyes were cool, clear green, but they were lifeless. Andy had never seen a dead person's eyes, but he imagined this was the way they'd look. He decided not to borrow the magazine and went back inside.

In the children's room, Marilyn was sitting at a table, reading a book called *Reptiles and How They Reproduce.* Andy had read it during the summer.

"I didn't know you like snakes," he said.

"I don't," said Marilyn. "I like to read." She looked up, and Andy was suddenly conscious of her green eyes. He started to tell her about the man in the courtyard, but she didn't act very friendly. He was about to leave, when she asked, "Do you like snakes?"

"Naw, not very much." Then he added, "I like to read, too," and they both laughed.

"I knew someone once who had a sixteen-foot python. Its cage was a screened porch."

"Where was that?"

"In California." She looked out the window as if she might be able to see it in the distance.

"You've been to California?"

"I lived there till we moved here."

"I've never been farther than North Carolina."

"Georgia's pretty," she said. "Maybe someday it'll seem like home."

"I was wondering if you'd like help with our homework in math?"

"Do you mean it?" said Marilyn. "You bet I would! I was going to put it off till tonight, but I'd sure be happy to get it over with now."

Andy had brought along his book and a notepad. "Here, use some of my paper," he said, opening his book to the assignment. It was on dividing large numbers, which Andy did not find difficult.

"Nothing about math is easy for me," said Marilyn, trying to work the first problem. He showed her where she'd used a wrong figure. Then they each worked the next problem, compared answers, and went on to the other problems. Whenever their answers did not agree, Andy would help her find whatever mistake she'd made. Once, a mistake had been his. "Oh, well," he said, smiling at her, "nobody's perfect."

"Sue Brady is," said Marilyn.

"You've noticed!"

"Does she ever make a mistake?"

Andy laughed. "Not that I know of. But don't let her or Patsy Dalton bother you. She thinks she's so smart, and Patsy thinks she's so pretty."

"Sue *is* smart," said Marilyn, "and Patsy's pretty." She looked at the clock over the checkout desk and stood up. "I have to go now. Thanks for the help." She gathered up her books and hurried out. Andy watched from the window as she walked across the parking lot and got into a cream-colored pickup truck, a Chevrolet El Camino that he had admired on his way in.

Andy remembered the time he thought he'd seen her riding in a limousine. He was glad now to see her getting into the pickup truck; it was somehow reassuring. It made her more like a lot of his friends. An El Camino was more streamlined and better-looking than most trucks, but at the same time it was no limousine.

He noticed the man in khaki work clothes and the cowboy hat walking across the parking lot but was surprised when he got into the El Camino and drove away. Surely that wasn't Marilyn's father. How could anyone so lifeless-looking be anyone's father? An older brother maybe; the man hadn't looked very old. Or a cousin. Or maybe no kin at all. A neighbor perhaps who was giving Marilyn a lift. It was only a coincidence that both had eyes the color of limeade.

At the next school assembly, Mr. Gray told the students how pleased he was with the response to the *Herald*'s poetry-writing contest. "There were so many interesting poems," he said, "that we had a hard time choosing. But we've finally selected the winner from Stokes, and the poem has gone to the paper as our official entry. Our winning poem was 'My Pets,' by Marilyn Peck, who is in the sixth grade and whose pen name for the contest is

Ruby Duff. Congratulations, Ruby Duff—and Marilyn! Stand up, will you, and let everyone know who you are."

Marilyn stood up.

Mr. Gray continued, "Tomorrow the *Herald* is sending out someone to take a picture of our young poet. Isn't that exciting?" Some of the students agreed that it was; others weren't so sure.

When they returned to their room, talk among the sixth-graders was of Marilyn's winning—and that the newspaper was sending a photographer to take her picture.

Emily asked, "Does that mean Ruby Duff has won the contest?"

"You mean Marilyn," corrected Mrs. Todd. "We must get back to calling her by her own name. And no, it doesn't mean she's the top winner, only that she's in the running. She represents our school. I expect the paper will be taking pictures of the winner from each school tomorrow."

"When will we know who won?" asked Dave.

"It's to be announced in next Friday's paper. Meanwhile, we'll all keep our fingers crossed for Ruby Duff. I'm sorry, Marilyn. I know you're Marilyn, not Ruby."

"Oh, that's all right. Maybe I'm both."

Patsy said, "If I were going to have my picture taken, I'd wear something pretty."

Emily turned to Marilyn. "Would you like to wear my new green sweater? It's got embroidery across the front."

"Oh, do!" said Louisa. "It'd be so pretty with your eyes."

"Thank you," said Marilyn. "But no. Thank you, anyway."

Mrs. Todd said, "A poet should be judged by what she writes, not what she wears."

Andy no longer thought of Marilyn as drab, but he knew everyone else did. Why did she wear such somber-looking clothes?

"Maybe she doesn't have anything to wear that's *in style,*" said Patsy.

"Well, there again, I'd disagree," said Mrs. Todd. "A poet is concerned with life as he or she sees it, not with what someone else thinks. I'd suggest we let Marilyn wear whatever she likes tomorrow."

The following morning Andy wondered if Mrs. Todd regretted making the suggestion. Marilyn arrived a few minutes late for school wearing the strangest thing he'd ever seen. It was over her coat; he supposed it was some kind of scarf. Whatever it was, it was made of pink feathers, and it was thrown around her neck and trailed almost to the floor.

"What's *that?*" asked Dave.

Marilyn looked indignant. "It's something to wear," she said.

"It's a *boa,*" said Mrs. Todd.

"Like a boa constrictor?" asked Rip.

"No, a feather boa. Perhaps it got its name because it's a snake-like wrap made of feathers or fur. They've been popular off and on for many years."

"Mostly *off* now," said Patsy.

"No, I saw a picture of one in a fashion magazine recently. They're never completely out of style. Although Marilyn may be the only student in Flag City to have worn one to school, she is, after all, to have her picture taken today. It's lovely, Marilyn."

"Thank you," said Marilyn. She put her books on her desk and carefully laid the boa across them. Then she took off her coat, and her outfit became even more interesting. Her dress glittered. It was made of red beads and sequins and looked as if it had been the top of a woman's evening gown. It was a bit loose-fitting, so she'd tightened it around the waist with a wide black belt with a buckle covered in rhinestones. The buckle was as big as a saucer.

Marilyn started to sit down, but evidently the buckle made sitting uncomfortable. She stood up and took off the belt. Holding out the buckle, she explained to Mrs. Todd and the class, "They're not real diamonds."

A Picture
in the Paper

On Friday afternoon, Mr. Gray stopped at Mrs. Todd's room during science class. "Could I interrupt for a moment?" he asked. Andy knew it must be something special; Mr. Gray almost never interrupted a class.

"Certainly, said Mrs. Todd, putting down the model of a dinosaur she'd been showing the class.

"Today's paper has just arrived," he said, "and I think your class should be the first to know the results of the poetry-writing contest. Marilyn Peck's poem has won the prize."

"Oh, that's wonderful!" said Mrs. Todd. Louisa and some of the other girls squealed.

"I'll leave the paper with you, and you can read it to the class," said Mr. Gray. He started out, and then turned back. "I'm proud of you, Marilyn." When he couldn't spot her, he looked puzzled.

"Here," said Marilyn, raising her hand. She had on a dress the color of the desk and wall paneling. No wonder Mr. Gray hadn't seen her, thought Andy. She was camouflaged. Mr. Gray congratulated her again and left.

Marilyn's picture was on the first page of the second half of the paper, the section called "People and Events." The photograph was in full color and took up half a page. The glittering dress and the feather boa were as dazzling in the picture as they'd actually been, thought Andy, but Marilyn looked different. In the picture, she was gazing into the distance as if she were in deep thought. Her eyes had a dreamy quality about them, and her other features appeared softer than they were. She looked almost pretty. No one would take her for the girl sitting near him now.

"Oh, that's a cute picture!" said Louise. "Marilyn, you look like a movie star!"

Karen said, "You look like you're thinking up a poem."

Patsy said, "There must not have been much other news today."

"Now, Patsy," scolded Mrs. Todd. "You must learn to be happy for other people."

"I'd have been happy if it'd been Sue," said Patsy, and Lena echoed her: "Yeah, so would I."

Karen, in the front row, squinted her eyes as she looked

at the photograph that Mrs. Todd held up and said, "Listen to what's underneath the picture: POETRY WINNER, MISS RUBY DUBB."

"Ruby *Duff*," said Dave. "Not Ruby *Dubb*."

"No," insisted Karen. "It says *Dubb,* D-u-b-b, doesn't it, Mrs. Todd?" Mrs. Todd looked at it. "Why, so it does. That's called a typographical error. Evidently the printer mistook the *f*s in the pseudonym for *b*s. Maybe we should have typed the entry instead of submitting it in your handwriting, Marilyn. Still, your penmanship is good; I don't know why the printer made such a mistake."

"It's all right,"said Marilyn. "It's an alias, anyway. Ruby Dubb sounds all right."

"Rubby-dub," said Rip, and Jason added: "Rubby-dub-dub, three men in a tub."

Mrs. Todd was still looking at the caption beneath the photo, and Dave asked, "What else does it say?"

"It says, 'For the identity of the winners, see page B5.' "

Sue said, "Then she wasn't the only winner."

"She was the *first-place* winner," said Mrs. Todd, a bit impatiently, as she turned to the fifth page of the section. "Yes, here's the poem. Let's see if the printer got it right." She read the poem aloud, and the students agreed that everything was as it should be.

"Does it say it's by Ruby Dubb?" asked Dave.

Looking at the page again, Mrs. Todd said, "Yes, it says *Dubb* again. At least they're consistent." Then she read the poems by the second- and third-place winners, who were from other schools. "And here's a short piece about the winners," said Mrs. Todd. "It says, 'The first prize, a leather-bound collection of *Favorite Poems, Old and New,* has been won by Marilyn Peck, who is in the sixth grade at Stokes Elementary School. Marilyn recently moved to Flag City from Saratoga, California. She makes her home in Garden Hills.' "

"Garden Hills!" It sounded as if every girl in the class and most of the boys had shouted it. Garden Hills was part of another world, thought Andy, even though it started just across the highway from the school. Nobody from there would be in this school. He'd seen children every now and then at Garden Hills—mostly in summer, sometimes on a weekend or over holidays. But he'd never thought of families really living there. He supposed permanent residents could have children; he'd just never thought of it.

Sue asked, "Does it really say *Garden Hills?*" Turning to Marilyn, she added, "I thought you lived on a farm."

"Yeah," said Dave. "How could anybody have room for a menagerie who didn't live out where there's lot of room?"

Marilyn said, "There's lots of room at Garden Hills." Andy knew that nobody could disagree; sometimes it seemed as if the resort were spread out over half the county.

Patsy said angrily, "I can't believe you live at Garden Hills. Just rich people live there."

Marilyn said softly, "Rich people can have pets."

The bell rang for the end of the school day, and students

gathered up their books and papers and hurried from the room.

Andy was walking with Jason toward the bike rack when he suddenly remembered that he was to ride the bus home. "I forgot," he said. "I'm not on my bike today. Dad dropped me off this morning." He turned and headed across the schoolyard. Patsy, Sue, and Lena were walking in the same direction. When he was near them, Patsy asked, "What'd you think about Marilyn being from Garden Hills?"

"I was surprised," said Andy. "What'd you think?"

"I thought anybody from Garden Hills would have a little more class."

"She had class in that newspaper picture," said Andy.

"Well, she doesn't anywhere else! She's dull-looking and stupid-acting." Andy had guessed that Patsy would be jealous, but he hadn't thought she'd be quite so upset.

"She's so quiet a lot of the time," said Sue, "that I figured she just wasn't friendly. But now we know it's because she's stuck-up."

"I wouldn't say that," said Andy.

"I would," said Sue. "She thinks she's better than the rest of us."

"She is better than the rest of us at writing poems," said Andy. He could see that his comment irritated Sue; he'd known it would. It was fun to remind her that for once somebody in their room had come out better than she had.

Andy went past the girls toward his bus. As he walked away, Patsy said, "Well, I don't like her."

"Me either," said Sue; and Lena, of course, echoed them: "Me either."

Monday morning Emily said, "My daddy laughed when he read Marilyn's poem in the paper. And he doesn't laugh much. He said we should elect Marilyn our poet laureate or something and ask her to write more poems."

"What's a poet laureate?" asked Blake.

"Someone chosen as the official poet of a nation or state or whatever," said Mrs. Todd. "I think it's a splendid idea that the sixth grade have one." She had let the class elect officers early in the term.

Blake said, "Then I nominate Ruby Dubb to be poet laureate of the sixth grade at Stokes Elementary School in Flag City, Georgia."

"Yea, Ruby Dubb!" yelled Jason, as if he were leading a cheer at a ball game. "Go, Poet Laureate!"

Almost everyone tried to say something then, and Mrs. Todd said, "All right! Settle down!" When the students didn't stop talking she said loudly: "All right! All right! Quiet down, or we won't do anything!" When everyone was quiet, she said, "Now, that's better. I'll permit you to have a business meeting for a few minutes, but only if you'll remember the rules of handling such matters. Who can tell me what was wrong with the way we just went about it?"

Andy said, "The session hadn't been officially declared open for business."

"It hadn't been officially declared a session," said Cal.

"Are we open for business now?" asked Louisa.

"No," said Mrs. Todd. "I'll call your president to the front of the room, and he'll take over." Matt started forward, and Mrs. Todd cautioned the class: "Now don't forget, he's the president that you elected, so if you're not going to be quiet while he's speaking, I'll have second thoghts about your being mature enough to have business sessions."

When Matt reached the front of the room, he said, "I declare the meeting open. Is there any business to discuss?"

"I make a motion that the class add a poet laureate to its elected officers," said Cal.

"Do I hear a second?"

He heard more than twenty of them when almost everyone said, "I second the motion."

Then he took a vote, and the motion carried unanimously. Next, he said, "The chair will hear nominations for the new office."

"I nominate Ruby Dubb," said Louisa.

"You mean Ruby *Duff,*" said Dave, and Karen said, "You mean Marilyn."

"May I say a word?" asked Mrs. Todd.

"You may," said Matt. "The chair recognizes Mrs. Todd."

"I'd suggest you ask Marilyn under which name she'd prefer to be known as the poet laureate."

"She's not the poet laureate yet," said Patsy. "The nominating's not over."

"In that case," said Mrs. Todd, "maybe ask Marilyn under what name she'd like to be nominated."

Marilyn said, "Ruby Dubb is all right with me if everybody else likes it."

Patsy said, "I nominate Sue Brady to be poet laureate."

Then someone made a motion, which was seconded, that the nominations be closed.

In the voting, done by secret ballot—pieces of paper folded and handed to the front—there were twenty-one votes for Ruby Dubb and three for Sue Brady.

Jason said, "Patsy demands a recount!" and everyone laughed but Patsy, Sue, and Lena.

At the end of the session, Dave said, "What exactly does a poet laureate do?"

"Write poems," said Jason. "What else?"

"I mean, when and what about?"

Mrs. Todd said, "Well, I hope Marilyn will write poems for us from time to time. She can write about things in her own life, or she might want to write about important things that happen here at school."

"Like our grade beating the seventh in softball?" asked Rip.

"Why not?" said Mrs. Todd.

"Write a poem about fat people, Marilyn," suggested Tubby Williams.

"Write another one about not having a dog," suggested Blake.

Marilyn said, "Maybe I'll write one about *having* a dog."

"You mean you have one now," asked Louisa. "Oh, that's wonderful." She sounded genuinely pleased.

Patsy, sounding genuinely sarcastic, said, "You're full of surprises. What else do you have that we don't know about?"

Marilyn looked at her. "If there's anything about me that I want everyone to know, I'll reveal it in a poem."

"Good idea," said Mrs. Todd. "And whenever you have a poem that you're willing to share with the rest of us, you may put it in the mailbox here on my desk at the end of the school day. If I feel that it's appropriate, I'll read it at the beginning of English class the next afternoon. How does that sound?"

"It sounds fine," said Marilyn. "Thank you." Turning to her classmates she smiled brightly and said, "And I thank all of you. I'll try not to disappoint you." Sometimes, thought Andy, even when she's wearing drab-colored clothes, she sparkles.

Big Bucky

Andy and Jason started home with Rip Larsen after school. All three boys had been anxious for this day to arrive. They were to visit the airport at Garden Hills. Rip's uncle, Harold Oakley, was manager and chief mechanic there. Since September he'd been promising the boys a tour of the hangar. Once before it had been planned, but something came up at the last moment, and it had to be canceled. Andy hoped nothing would go wrong this time.

The boys were riding their bikes to Rip's house. Later in the afternoon, his mother would drive them to the airstrip. It seemed a long way around—the hangar was just across the highway from school—but Mr. Oakley thought it best that they wait until late afternoon to make the visit. By then, unless something unexpected came up, the work would be finished for the day, and everyone else would have gone home. They'd have the place to themselves. Besides, Rip's mother wanted to go with them and see the hangar and the fine planes that her younger brother worked on.

It was a beautiful fall afternoon, and as there was plenty of time, they took the road alongside Garden Hills that went past one of the lakes. The last time Andy and Rip had been there, they'd seen a great blue heron wading in shallow water. While they'd stood watching, it had caught a big fish, tossed it about on the ground a few times, then swallowed it. They'd been amazed at what a large fish it could get down its skinny throat.

Rip steered his bike onto the shoulder of the road and stopped. "Let's see if we spot the heron," he said.

"Probably it's started south by now," said Andy. "If I had wings, I'd be at St. Simon's Island." He and his family had spent a week there last summer.

"I'd rather be at Jekyll," said Jason. St. Simon's and Jekyll were islands off the Georgia coast.

No heron was in sight, but a kingfisher flew into a tall sweetgum tree. It lit on a branch that hung out over the lake. While they were looking at it, it dropped headfirst into the water like a dive bomber. Immediately it came out of the water and flew away. They couldn't tell if it had caught a fish or not. While they waited to see if it would come back, Jason pointed toward the houses near the top of the hill. "Look up there!"

"That's where Garden Hills folks live," said Andy. "The permanent residents."

"No, I mean that big dog." Andy and Rip saw it, too. The dog was frolicking in an open area between two houses. They could see it through the trees. "That's what I'd call one-more-big-dog," said Rip. "What kind is it?"

"A St. Bernard," said Andy. He'd been reading a book about the dog breeds from the library at school that Blake had recommended. Some of Blake's relatives raised dogs.

Although the St. Bernard was big, it bounced around as playfully as a puppy. It would run a short way, turn around and run back. Then it would go off in a different direction.

"Say," said Rip, "there's Lester Cato!" Lester, an eighth-grader, was the brother of their classmate Dave. He was really too far away for them to have recognized him, but they knew he had an afternoon paper route through Garden Hills.

The big dog noticed Lester at the same time they did and chased after him. It ran past the bicycle and then suddenly turned back. It jumped into the air and then flopped onto the ground—its front legs out flat and spread apart as if they were open arms waiting for the boy and the bike to rush into them. Its tail was sticking high in the air.

The boys laughed. Lester turned around quickly. The

dog hopped up and ran after him and did the same thing again, blocking his way. After doing this two more times, instead of running past Lester and blocking him again, the dog loped alongside the bike for a moment. Then it grabbed Lester by the seat of the pants. Lester managed to stop the bike without falling off. Next, the dog tugged at his pants leg, pulling him along. Just then a girl came running up, waving her arms at the dog, and Lester was set free.

"The show's over," said Rip, starting ahead. He looked back at Andy. "Come on, King Kong, we've gotta go."

Andy said, "That girl looked like Marilyn." He pushed his bike onto the road.

"It probably was," agreed Jason. "I doubt there are many other kids who live up there."

"Speed it up, you guys," called Rip.

Jason and Andy hurried along. They certainly didn't want to miss this chance to visit the airstrip.

Mrs. Larsen greeted the boys warmly, and after she'd served each of them a big wedge of pecan pie—and a small piece for her—everyone sat down at the kitchen table. When they'd finished the refreshments Rip collected the dishes and reached over and put them in the sink. His mother said, "Your Uncle Harold was to call if anything came up so that he couldn't show us around." She looked at her watch. "And I haven't heard from him, so we'll assume all systems are go. Is everybody ready?"

The boys hopped up and were racing toward the car when the telephone rang. A moment later Mrs. Larsen called them back inside. "Oh, no," said Rip. "Don't tell us it's been canceled again."

"I'm afraid so."

Jason said, "And this was going to be the highlight of my life."

"You and Andy are still invited to spend the night," said Mrs. Larsen. "And there's a big lasagne in the oven. Who knows, supper may turn out to be the highlight of everybody's life!"

At the beginning of the English lesson, Mrs. Todd said, "Our poet laureate has written a poem, so we'll take a few minutes now to see what we think of it." Andy had seen Marilyn drop a poem in Mrs. Todd's mailbox the afternoon before.

"It's called 'Big Bucky,'" said Mrs. Todd, and she read:

> She's very big, my St. Bernard
> And off to a lively start,
> Although it's true she's almost grown
> She's still a puppy in her heart.
>
> Her real name's Bucknell of Elsonia,
> But we call her Bucky today.
> She came from the Silicon Valley
> In California, U.S.A.
>
> She flew here by airplane
> A yellow one called Daisy.

My friend, the owner, told me,
    On the way she drove him crazy.

She started out so sweetly,
    A nice and gentle pup,
Then while he wasn't looking,
    She chewed the compass up.

My father doesn't like her;
    She ate his golfing shoes.
He says she's more destructive
    Than a dozen wrecking crews.

She once jumped over a sofa,
    A table, a lamp, and a chair,
Into a cupboard of dishes
    She didn't know was there.

So now she is an *outdoor* dog
    Yet still she's pulling capers
Like barking at the passersby
    And dragging in newspapers.

Her playfulness brings trouble;
    To her, no doubt, it's joy.
One day she barked at passersby
    And dragged in the paper boy.

Andy noticed that Marilyn looked especially happy when everyone laughed. She didn't laugh herself, but she smiled as she looked around the room at everyone else laughing.

Dave said angrily, "That was my brother! He said that while he was delivering the papers the other day, a big ol' dog came running out and nearly knocked him down. Then it grabbed him by his pants and wouldn't let him go."

"That's the way it was," said Jason. "Me and Andy and Rip saw ol' Lester get caught."

"Did the dog bite him?" asked Matt.

"Scared him half to death," complained Dave.

Marilyn spoke up. "Bucky just wanted to play. And she did *not* bite him."

"He said he yelled for help," continued Dave, "and that a *weird-looking* girl came running up. I didn't know it was you."

Marilyn looked for a moment as if someone had slapped her, but when her classmates laughed more about a dog snagging a paper boy, she cheered up.

Cal told Dave, "I bet you could have heard your brother yelling all the way across town."

Marilyn laughed then. "Yes," she said, "you could have! And the louder he yelled, the more Bucky tugged at his pants leg, sort of pulling him along. When I told her to cut it out, she stopped and jumped up and licked him on the face."

Cal said, "I rode with my father on Saturday, and we saw that whopper of a dog." His father owned a truck and hauled garbage for areas that weren't covered by the city's routes. Garden Hills was one of his main customers. Turning to Marilyn, Cal said, "I didn't see you, but your dog was having a good time playing. An old man and woman were throwing a Frisbee for it to try to catch. And I never saw such a critter! Why, it's as big as a Shetland pony!"

"Maybe it *is* a Shetland pony," said Jason. "That could be a poem for you, Marilyn: 'My Dog Turned Out To Be a Horse.'"

Marilyn laughed along with everyone else, and when there was quiet again, Andy noticed that she was gazing into the distance as if she weren't really paying close attention now to what was going on around her. "It's funny," she said, "I've never had a horse."

Matt asked, "Do you really know the owner of the Yellow Daisy?"

"What?" she said, suddenly back from her dream world. "The Yellow Daisy? Daisy, the airplane? Yes, I know him."

Louisa asked, "Is he really a Hollywood producer or something?"

"No," said Marilyn.

"Oh," said Patsy, "we thought he was a big rich man."

"He has a plant in the Silicon Valley that makes computer stuff," explained Marilyn.

"Wow!" said Cal. "Silicon Valley! When I get to be an engineer, that's where I'm heading. If your friend's in computers there, he's gotta be wealthy."

"Maybe he is," said Marilyn. "He has a nice home in California that's on the Pacific Ocean, and he owns one at Garden Hills that he uses whenever he brings his family out here. He may be rich, but money's not what's important. He's a fine man, that's what matters."

"How come you know him?" asked Lena.

"He and my father were roommates in college. Later on, they started a business together."

"Is your father still in business with him?"

Before Marilyn could answer, Mrs. Todd said, "I expect that's enough now. Marilyn, I think you can tell that your poem was appreciated and enjoyed. We thank you. Now if all of you will open your books we'll get on with irregular verbs."

On the way out of the building after school, Andy turned to Marilyn. "I saw that big dog again yesterday when I was riding my bike out your way. It looked like you playing with her, but I couldn't tell for sure. You were down by the edge of the lake."

"Why didn't you stop and play with us?" she asked.

Andy laughed. "Well, for one thing, there's a six-foot cyclone fence in the way. And for another, there are three strands of barbed wire across the top of it."

"Yes, I know," said Marilyn. "My father calls that 'forbidding.' I wish there were a gate along there."

Andy didn't remind her that the gates of Garden Hills that weren't securely locked were manned by guards. Soon after the resort had opened, he and Rip had gone there to ride their bikes through the grounds. Guards at the main gate had thrown them out so quickly that they hadn't tried again.

Marilyn started across the school grounds, then turned

and called back, "If you see me down there again, call good and loud. I'll bring Bucky over to the fence; she'd like to meet you."

Andy watched as Marilyn went over to the curb where vehicles were waiting. She got into the El Camino pickup with the green-eyed man in the cowboy hat. The man did not smile or even appear to speak to her as they drove away. Andy still hoped it wasn't her father.

A Learjet
and an
Arabian Horse

The Garden Hills gate nearest the airstrip was locked at night. In the daytime it remained open but was guarded. "Yes, ma'am," said the guard, when Mrs. Larsen had explained why they were there, "your brother told me you'd be coming." He directed them to a parking lot off to the side. At least, thought Andy, we've gotten this far.

As they were getting out of the car, they saw Rip's Uncle Harold standing outside the hangar, talking to a man who had one foot propped on a golf cart. Andy supposed he'd driven it through the woods from the clubhouse. Trails were everywhere in Garden Hills. The boys stopped at an open door of the hangar and looked inside at the planes parked on the ramp. Harold called, "Come on out here. I want you to meet someone." When they were all together, he introduced the man as Mr. Charley Berry. "This is my sister, Nancy Larsen," he said. "And her good-for-nothing son, my nephew, ol' Rip here." He tousled Rip's hair and gave him a bear hug.

Mrs. Larsen said, "And these are our friends, Jason and Andy."

"Glad to meet you," said Mr. Berry, sounding as if he meant it. He shook hands with each one of them.

"They're wanting to see the hangar, and I've been promising them a conducted tour," said Harold. "I think they're planning to be the world's greatest pilots someday."

Mr. Berry laughed. "Maybe they'll outgrow the notion," he said, smiling at Mrs. Larsen. "At the moment, my children are planning to be the world's greatest acrobats."

"What children have you?" she asked.

"Two girls and a boy. All younger than these three." He gave Andy a friendly pat on the shoulder and got into the golf cart. "Let me get out of the way so the tour can begin. Thanks, Harold, for the help."

"Anytime," said Harold.

After he'd driven the cart a short distance across the parking lot, Mr. Berry turned and called back. "Take them aboard my plane if you think they'd be interested in seeing inside it."

"I'm sure they would," said Harold. "Thank you very much." The boys had been told not to expect to go aboard any of the planes, as the owners did not like for anyone except authorized personnel to touch them.

"Which one's his?" asked Rip, excitedly.

"A little yellow one inside." Andy had noticed the Piper Tomahawk parked next to the Yellow Daisy. His sister Dru would have declared them a mother airplane and a baby airplane.

"What a nice man," said Mrs. Larsen. "Where does he live?"

"California. But he spends a lot of time out here. He's one of the main investors in the resort." He held the door open for everyone to go inside.

"This is the sheet-metal shop," said Harold, stopping to point out some of the equipment in the hangar. "That monster over there's for cutting pieces of metal when we make skin repairs."

"Skin repairs!" said Mrs. Larsen in a shocked tone.

Harold reached across and rubbed a finger up and down her arm. "The outside of a plane," he said. "You know, skin!"

She laughed as she slapped his hand away.

"But all of 'em are not metal," he said. "Some of the smaller planes are covered with a kind of cloth. Come on, I'll show you our dope and fabric area." He explained that dope was a resin-type mix that shrank and hardened until it was almost as tough as metal, yet lightweight.

He took them through other shops where repairs were made, including the one where engines were overhauled. "Now for the ramp," he said.

This was what the boys had looked forward to most of

all. They'd read books and magazines about aircraft—all they could find, in fact, in the school and public library. But reading about the planes and seeing them were two different things, thought Andy. He couldn't remember when he'd been more excited about anything.

Harold stopped at each plane on the ramp and gave the boys a chance to walk around it. The boys' favorites were not all in, but quite a few of them were. At the blue-and-white Cessna Skyhawk, the one they'd named the "Jaybird," Harold called their attention to its landing gear. "It has a nose wheel instead of a tail dragger," he pointed out. When they inspected a Gulfstream II, he said, "Gulfstreams are made here in Georgia."

"Where?" asked Mrs. Larsen.

"Savannah. They have a big plant down there."

There were other planes—an Aero Commander, a Cessna Citation, and a Piper Cherokee were of special interest to the boys, as they'd seen all three landing earlier that day.

By then, there were only two planes left—the Yellow Daisy and, at the end, the smaller Piper Tomahawk. It came to Andy that "Canary" would be a good name for the Tomahawk.

At the Yellow Daisy, Andy said, "This one's our favorite."

"Mine too," said Harold, standing near the front of it. He reached up, turned a handle, and opened the door. It swung down, and the inside of the door became part of the steps.

"Ladies first!" he said, with a sweeping gesture to his sister. Andy knew he was joking, but still, it was fun to see the plane with its door open. Mrs. Larsen didn't move, and Harold insisted: "Come on! Mr. Berry invited us."

"Mr. Berry!" shouted Rip. "You mean this is his plane? You said his was the little yellow one."

"I was kidding," said Harold. "I meant the big yellow one. Yep, Mr. Berry is the owner of this baby." He patted the Learjet lovingly. "It's the Cadillac of private planes."

Mrs. Larsen went up the steps. "Up and to the right," directed Harold. "We'll see the cabin first."

When they were inside, Mrs. Larsen said, "My goodness, this is like a comfortable living room." She looked around at the handsome furniture.

"Yep," agreed Harold, "but they're not all alike. If you can afford a Learjet, you can afford to have the interior designed to suit yourself. But what do you say we check out the cockpit?"

The boys hurried toward the front. Rip got there first and sat down in the pilot's seat, and Andy took the co-pilot's place. An instrument panel was in front of each one with a boxlike cabinet on the floor between them. "That's called the pedestal," said Harold, when he noticed Andy looking at it. "The main thing in it's the radio." He leaned across to the panel in front of Andy and began to explain what the buttons and knobs on it controlled. Andy was careful not to touch anything, but Rip fidgeted with everything. Suddenly bells began to ring, and red lights blinked on across both panels.

Mrs. Larsen screamed, "Rip, what have you done? Harold, quick, do something!"

Rip looked frantic. "What'd I do? What's wrong?" he asked.

"I don't know," said Harold. "Don't blow us up!" Then he began to laugh. Andy noticed that Harold's thumb was holding down a button on the panel. When he lifted his thumb, the commotion ended.

"Just thought I'd see if anybody's awake," said Harold. He reached over and touched a similar button on the panel in front of Rip. "It's for a fire-warning test," he explained.

"You scared me to death," said Mrs. Larsen. "But I'm ready to have my turn at flying a Learjet. Rip, you and Andy get up and let the experts take over. Jason, you be the pilot, and I'll assist."

While they traded places, Harold continued to explain what the various controls were used for. When he leaned across Jason to the panel in front of him, Andy suspected that he was going to set off the bells and lights again. He did press one of the buttons, but a different one this time, and a voice, sounding like a robot, said, "Whoop, whoop, pull up! Whoop, whoop, pull up!" Then: "Glide slope . . . glide slope."

"That's the Ground-Prox button," explained Harold, when he'd released it. "Prox for proximity, meaning the proximity to the ground—in other words, how close you are to it."

Rip said, "I heard a voice like that in a car at the automobile show." He imitated the sound: "Fasten your seat belt. Fasten your seat belt."

"Yes," said Mrs. Larsen, "but 'Whoop! Whoop! Pull up' sounds so silly."

"It wouldn't if you were flying along and suddenly you were heading over a mountain or something. Or if you were about to come down and didn't have your landing gear ready."

"Okay, okay, I'm convinced," said Mrs. Larsen. Glancing at her watch, she added, "And we'd better be going."

"Not yet!" pleaded Rip, and his mother stood by while Harold explained more about the Learjet to the boys.

After a while, Mrs. Larsen said firmly that it was time to go, and the boys thanked Harold for the great time they'd had. Andy said, "It was even better than we'd thought it would be."

There were no planes on the runway Monday morning, and conversation among the boys at recess turned to other things. Cal told them about riding through Garden Hills again on Saturday on his father's garbage truck. "You ought to've seen Marilyn," he said.

"Was she playing with that big St. Bernard again?" asked Rip.

"No, she was riding a horse. The prettiest one I've ever seen."

"What kind was it?" asked Matt. He lived out in the country, and he and his sisters had a horse. Also, their father boarded horses for other people. Matt helped look after them.

"It was an Arabian," said Cal. "I've only seen them in pictures, but I'm sure that's what it was. And was it ever a beauty!"

Matt asked, "What color was it?"

"Light gray," said Cal, "with a black mane and tail."

On the way back into the building, Matt spoke to Marilyn about it. "Cal saw you riding a good-looking horse. He thinks it was an Arabian."

"Yes, that's what it was."

"Wow!" said Matt. "You're lucky! Where'd you get it?"

Andy caught a glimpse of Marilyn's expression as she answered; he thought she looked the least bit worried. "I'll wait and reveal it in a poem," she said. Then, as if she'd given a shorter answer than she'd meant, she added, "I'm turning in a poem about it this afternoon, okay?"

"Sure," said Matt, "that's okay," and on Tuesday afternoon Mrs. Todd read the poem to the class:

> "A *real* tiger!" said my father,
>   "You're as crazy as can be!
> No, you may not have one,
>   Now please don't bother me."
>
> "An elephant!" said my father,
>   "What's come over you?
> We'd need to hire a keeper,
>   And that we cannot do."

"A zebra?" said my father,
      "You mean, a zebra for a pet?
Ridiculous! Impossible!
      Your worst idea yet!"

"How about a lion?" I asked,
      Of course, he answered, "No."
"A rhino?" "A hippo?" "A giraffe?"
      "No," "No," and, "No."

"What if you had a horse?" he said,
      "And perhaps a riding ring?"
I promised I'd quit asking then
      For another living thing!

Mrs. Todd was called to the office just as she finished the poem. "You may discuss it among yourselves," she said as she was leaving, "but keep your voices down."

After she was out of the room, Emily said, "It must be nice to be rich and live in Garden Hills."

"Yes," said Louisa. "You'd barely finished saying you'd never had a dog when suddenly a big, beautiful St. Bernard was flown out to you from California. And then you just mentioned that you'd never had a horse, and now you have one."

Karen asked, "Do you always get everything you ask for?"

"Why, no, of course not," said Marilyn. "I didn't get a tiger, did I? Or a lion?"

"Or a zebra!" added Blake. "It'd be fun to have a zebra."

Jason said, "Yeah. Giddy-up, giddy-up, Striped Horsie!"

Everyone appeared happy for Marilyn except Patsy, Sue, and Lena—and maybe Dave, who seldom appeared happy about anything. Sue asked Marilyn, "What'd you name the horse—Spot or Fido?"

Everyone laughed then but Dave. Marilyn said, "No, they were named before they got here. I mean, it already had a name. She's called Dolly."

Mrs. Todd came back into the room. "I'm going to talk about tenses of verbs," she said. "And if you'll pay close attention, and ask questions about anything you don't understand, maybe I won't assign any homework. Is that all right?"

Everyone agreed that it was indeed all right. School was letting out that afternoon for the rest of the week for Thanksgiving.

Andy was glad not to have any books to take home. On weekends and holidays, his mother insisted that he do his homework ahead of anything else. When he didn't have homework this time, she let him ride his bike out to Rip's house.

They played with Rip's rocket launcher for a while and then rode their bikes over to Blake's house to see some bullterrier puppies. The puppies belonged to Blake's cousin, who was also his next-door neighbor.

On the way home, Rip turned off to go to his house, and Andy took the road that went past Garden Hills. He hoped to see Marilyn out riding her horse, and at the end of the lake, he stopped and got off his bike. He crossed the shoulder of the road and stood next to the fence. At first he didn't see her, but soon Marilyn came along a trail even nearer the fence than the one down by the lake. He called to her, and she rode over to him.

"Say," he said, "that *is* a pretty horse!"

"She's sweet, too," said Marilyn. "Pat her on the forehead; she likes that." Then she laughed. "I'm sorry. I keep forgetting about the fence that separates us." She got off the horse and led Dolly as close as possible to Andy.

"How does the dog like her?" asked Andy.

"They'll get used to each other. We're letting Dolly settle into her new surroundings before we risk putting Bucky near her. Bucky might scare Dolly; Dolly might kick Bucky. You know."

"When I got home from school a while ago," said Andy, "my mother reminded me that our family's having some friends from church over on Friday. She said I could invite some of my friends if I'd care to. Would you like to come?"

"Oh, thank you," said Marilyn. "I'd like to, if I can." She thought a moment and said, "No, that's the Friday after Thanksgiving Day. No, I can't come." When Andy looked disappointed, she said, "Some of our friends are coming, too. I was forgetting: the Yellow Daisy is due in tomorrow for the rest of the week. But thank you, anyway."

Just then, a man on another Arabian horse—this one a bay—came riding out toward them. He'd come from a cluster of low buildings that had recently been completed. During the fall, Andy had noticed the buildings under construction whenever he'd gone to Rip's.

"Are those stables?" he asked.

"Yes," answered Marilyn, just as the man drew near. He had on khaki work clothes. He didn't notice Andy, but he smiled at Marilyn and said in an English accent, "This one's my favorite. But I think we'll get along fine with all of them." He pulled in the reins and the horse stopped. "Hal had to drive up to Atlanta to pick up a load of grass seed for the golf courses," said the man. "He said to tell you that he might be late getting back and for you to open a can of Vienna sausage or eat a bowl of cereal for supper." Then he noticed Andy. "Oh, hello," he said. "I didn't see you here." Andy was standing among tall weeds. "With your green sweater, you blend in with the undergrowth. Is there something you wanted?"

Marilyn said, "He's a friend of mine from school. He was riding his bike past, and I stopped him."

"I see," said the man, turning back to Marilyn. "Well, I expect we'd better get on with our work. When you put Dolly in her stall, rub her down, but don't feed her. Then bring out Rusty for a little gallop. She needs the exercise. Then rub her down. I'll be back soon with Ginger, and we'll feed all of them when they've rested a bit." Nodding stiffly to Andy, he said, "Excuse us, young man." He gave the horse a slight nudge with his knees, saying, "Git up now, Ginger!" and rode away.

"I'd better go," said Marilyn, mounting Dolly. "Happy Thanksgiving!"

June-bug

Twice during Thanksgiving break, Andy rode his bike past Garden Hills. Once he didn't see Marilyn at all. The other time, she was at the swings near the tennis courts at the top of the hill. He didn't call to her as she was playing with three other children—two little girls and a boy who was hardly more than a toddler.

Marilyn was the only one who was swinging. The two girls were turning cartwheels and doing handstands in front of her, while the little boy did a balancing act on the top rail of the swing set. Andy hoped he wouldn't fall.

Whenever one of the girls did a really nice cartwheel or handstand, Marilyn clapped her hands and the girl would take a bow as if she'd performed a marvelous acrobatic stunt. When the boy climbed down the side of the swing set to the ground, he went running to Marilyn. She held a tissue for him to blow his nose.

On Monday morning after the holiday, Andy had thought he saw the same three children getting into the Yellow Daisy just before it took off. Two days later, he was surprised by a poem of Marilyn's that Mrs. Todd read to the class. It was called "My Two Little Sisters and Our Baby Brother, June-bug." "It's by Ruby Dubb," said Mrs. Todd, and she read the poem:

My sisters are Lori and Anna Marie,
    They're younger than I by a number of years.
June-bug's the baby, he's tough as can be
    He'll fight you or bite you; there's nothing he fears.

He has red hair and freckles—sometimes a black eye—
    And bruises all over from places he's bumped.
He climbed a pecan tree and went really high;
    I called, "Be careful!" He shouted, "Catch me!"
        and jumped.

Bucky our dog's not the least bit obedient
    Whenever I call her, my call is not heeded,
But when June-bug calls her she finds it expedient
    To come in a hurry to see what is needed.

All of us humor him, no one refuses.
    We chase after June-bug wherever he goes.

At bedtime I read to him books that he chooses;
   If a story ends badly, he punches my nose.

I'm glad to have sisters; we have fun with each other,
   And both of them tell me they're glad to have me.
We agree that we're lucky to have us a brother,
   If there were no June-bug how dull it would be.

After she'd read it, Mrs. Todd said, "We'll take a few moments to discuss this poem. If you liked it, you may say so; if you didn't, you may do the same. I feel sure that our poet laureate will welcome objective criticism of her work. Dave, we'll let you be first. Tell us how you truly feel about it—and why."

"It had too many big words in it," said Dave.

Rip said, "Naw, it didn't have too many big words."

"It did so," insisted Dave.

"Like what?"

"Like *obedient*."

"*Obedient!*" snapped Rip. "Why, I hear that all the time." Imitating his mother, he said, "You *will be* obedient, or I'll know the reason why!" Andy laughed. More than once he had heard her say it to Rip in just that way.

"Well, *expedient* then. That's a big word."

Jason said, "It's *expedient* that you be *obedient!*"

Mrs. Todd asked Dave if he remembered a lesson on picking up clues about what a word meant from the way it was used. "What's that called?"

Dave didn't know, and Mrs. Todd said, "If nobody

remembers, we'll have that lesson again!"

Sue, as always, knew the answer: "It's called using context clues. You get hints of one word's meaning from other words and phrases."

"Very good," said Mrs. Todd. "And Dave, after you've come across *expedient* a few more times, you'll know it forever. Now, let's get back to the poem."

Blake said, "Well, it was funny in places, but it got too sweet at the end. I liked all but the last verse."

"Yeah," said Lena. "I thought the whole thing was yucky."

"I'll let you by this time with using slang, provided you tell us why you thought it was yucky."

"Well, nobody likes their brothers and sisters," said Lena, as if she were stating an absolute fact.

"I do," said Louisa. "I like both my brothers fine."

"That's 'cause they're a lot older than you," said Lena, "and they don't get in your way."

"I like my brother okay," said Blake. "It's his wife I could do without."

"Now, Blake," scolded Mrs. Todd, "let's have no more about your new sister-in-law. Karen, what did you think of the poem?"

Karen said, "I liked it, but maybe not quite as much as some of Marilyn's other ones. Maybe that's because I'd really rather play with friends my own age than my little brothers and my sister."

"Yeah, me, too," said Emily. "Wouldn't you, Marilyn? Honestly, wouldn't you?"

Marilyn said, "But I have friends my own age," which Andy didn't think made much sense. Quickly Marilyn added, "I mean, it's nice to have friends *and* a family."

Cal said, "If my little brother behaved like June-bug, my mother would blister his behind."

"I was thinking the same thing," said Patsy. "Marilyn, what does your mother say about the way June-bug behaves?"

Marilyn answered, "She doesn't say anything."

Mrs. Todd said, "Marilyn, didn't your records indicate that your mother is dead?"

Marilyn looked up, her face turning a bit red. Then she said calmly, "Yes, ma'am, she is."

"Maybe that's why she doesn't say anything!" said Jason, and Mrs. Todd told him that his remark was inappropriate.

Patsy said, "Well, Marilyn's was inappropriate, too. I wouldn't have asked what her mother had said if I'd known she wasn't living. Anytime we ask Marilyn anything, she says, 'I'll reveal it in a poem if I want you to know.' Well, if she would act like a normal person, we'd have known her mother was dead."

"That's enough, that's enough," said Mrs. Todd sternly. "I thought we'd use the poem for a brief discussion, and I'm sorry if I steered it in a personal direction. I hadn't meant to. But we *will not* dwell on personalities. Is that clear?" It was so clear that no one said anything for a moment.

"I didn't think it was very smooth," said Sue.

Emily disagreed, "I thought it was," and Louisa

said, "Mrs. Todd, what did you think of it?"

"Yeah," said Rip. "Tell us how you truly feel about it—and why."

That put Mrs. Todd in a better humor. "Well, the criticism that it isn't smooth has some merit. There are lines that don't quite fit. But the poem has a slightly different rhythm than our poet laureate's earlier efforts, and I hope she'll keep trying new patterns. As for how I truly felt otherwise, I found the poet's love of family rather touching." Smiling at Rip, she asked, "Did I do all right? Did I tell you how I truly felt?"

Before Rip could answer, the secretary's voice came over the intercom, asking Mrs. Todd if she would bring her register to Mr. Gray. It had something to do with attendance records.

While Mrs. Todd was out, Louisa said to Marilyn, "I'm sorry your mother's dead."

"What about your father?" asked Patsy, and Lena added, "Maybe he's dead, too."

"No! No! No, he's not!" Marilyn practically screamed it. Her mouth twitched and she sniffed. Andy thought for a moment that she was going to cry. "My father's not dead!" she said again. "My father's not dead."

Anybody else would have let the subject drop, thought Andy, but Patsy continued. Mimicking Marilyn, she said, "Perhaps you'll *reveal him* in a poem."

Marilyn glared at her. Although she still looked upset, she said calmly, "Perhaps I will."

Christmas Shopping

On a Saturday in early December Andy went shopping downtown with his mother and Dru. His mother had insisted that he come along. They were to browse in one of the big stores and get ideas for toys and games that appealed to Dru. Then Andy was to take Dru out of the store while his mother did the shopping.

"Come on, Dru," said Andy, when his mother had whispered that by now she had enough ideas about things Dru liked. "Let's go window-shopping. It's too crowded in here."

"Good idea!" said Mrs. Haley. "You two run along, and I'll meet you at the Buzzard's Roost at eleven-thirty." The long bench outside the Garden Center at the end of the block was called the Buzzard's Roost.

"I don't like to window-shop," said Dru.

"Aw, come on!" urged Andy. "There's a giant Santa Claus in the window of the card shop."

"I've seen it."

Mrs. Haley said, "Run on with your brother now." She winked at Andy and added, "I need to go to housewares to buy some pots and pans. You'd be bored."

"I like pots and pans," said Dru.

Handing two dollars to Andy, Mrs. Haley said, "Maybe you should have ice cream at Baskin-Robbins."

"I'm going," said Andy, "whether Dru comes or not." He started away, and after he'd passed only two counters, Dru came running after him. He'd known she would. "Wait a minute!" she yelled. "I'm coming."

They went first for the ice cream, then moseyed along the sidewalk, stopping whenever a display caught their eye. Soon they were at the Garden Center. As usual, there were wheelbarrows on display out front. Dru always had to test each one to see if she was big enough to push it. Andy sat down on the Buzzard's Roost and waited. While he was there, he noticed an El Camino pickup parked alongside the loading ramp near the end of the building. And it was cream-colored. He wondered if it was the same one he'd seen Marilyn riding in. A clerk near it was assembling an order—two shovels, three rakes, a bush blade, a chain saw—and three leaf shredders. Andy couldn't imagine anyone needing three leaf shredders. He and Dru and his mother were giving his father one for Christmas. Then he saw the tall man in the cowboy hat; he was talking to the clerk.

Dru wanted to see if there were more wheelbarrows inside, and Andy followed her into the store. Off to one side, he spotted Marilyn browsing in the plant section.

At this time of year, the main plants in the store were shrubs and trees for fall planting. But there were two long tables of poinsettias and Christmas greenery and another of assorted house plants. Marilyn stood at the third one, examining a small pot plant with pink blooms. She looked up when Andy spoke to her. Instead of saying hello, she asked, "Do you suppose these really grow in the woods in Africa?"

Andy laughed. "I don't *really* have any idea."

At that, Marilyn laughed, too. "They're African violets. I've heard that they grow wild in African forests." She put the plant down just as Dru rushed up, saying, "I've decided what I most want Santa Claus to bring me."

"Is that your sister?"

"Yeah. Dru."

Dru looked up. "Dru, for Drucilla," she said.

"Hi," said Marilyn. Then she asked Andy, "Aren't you going to ask what she most wants?"

"Yeah," said Dru. "Ask me."

"I know."

"No, you don't."

"Yes, I do. And Santa Claus ain't gonna bring a

five-year-old girl a real wheelbarrow."

"He might," snapped Dru. "You don't know." She ran off to look at a big garden cart.

Marilyn turned from the violets to a tray of waxy-leaved plants with yellow blossoms. The man in the cowboy hat came over to a counter nearby and picked up a pair of lopping shears. Marilyn called across to him, "Look, Dad!" She took one of the plants from the tray and held it up. "This is the first time I've seen these in Georgia."

Andy was almost sorry to know for certain that the man was her father. He didn't know why exactly except that the man was somehow different. Woebegone, Andy's mother would have called him.

To Andy, Marilyn said, "These grow outdoors in California." Then, to her father again, "Aren't they nice? Let's buy one."

Her father looked at the plant a moment. "Let's don't," he said. He put down the shears and walked away. Andy was thinking that he must be close with his money when Mr. Peck turned and came back. He handed Marilyn a five-dollar bill. "Buy a plant. But not one of those, okay?" He turned and walked away again.

Marilyn put down the pot she'd been holding. Andy was puzzled. "What's he got against those plants?"

"My mother had a border of them around our patio. She loved to work with flowers." Marilyn looked at the plants in the tray. "I suppose they reminded him too much of her." She stared at the flowers longer, then said, "Even though it makes me sad, I like to see things and have things that remind me of her. With him, it's the other way."

"Didn't they get along?" After he'd said it, Andy realized that maybe he shouldn't have.

Marilyn looked shocked. Andy was afraid he'd offended her. But when she continued, she didn't seem annoyed. "They'd been in love since they were in junior high school," she said. "Dad nearly went crazy after she died." She lowered her voice and added, "In fact, he did . . . sort of. But he'd been nearly down before that, worrying about business problems and all. Anyway, he had a bad breakdown and was in the hospital for a long time. It was scary."

"What'd you do while he was sick?"

"He's still sick."

A scene at school flashed through Andy's mind: the time someone had said that perhaps her father was dead, and she'd screamed out that he wasn't. "I mean, while he was in the hospital?"

"I lived with the Berrys. You met Charley Berry, the owner of the Yellow Daisy, didn't you?"

"Yeah, he let Rip and Jason and me go on his plane."

"Well, he arranged for Dad to come here. The doctors had ordered a change till he's stronger, and Charley Berry worked it out for Dad to oversee the grounds crew for the golf courses and all. Hard work out in the fresh air was supposed to help him."

"Has it?"

"I don't know." She looked sad, and Andy didn't know

what to say. Then Marilyn smiled. "I wish you'd known him in the old days. And Mom, too." She spoke hurriedly now, as if telling about the way they used to be might somehow make everything right again. "They were on the equestrian team of the Olympics the year they got out of college. Of course, I wasn't around then."

"Wow!" said Andy. "Then it really was your father's idea to get the horses."

"No, it wasn't. Charley thought it might help Dad and that it would be good for the resort at the same time. But Dad hasn't been much interested in them. Or anything else. But I hadn't meant to talk so much. Would you do me a favor?"

"Sure."

"Don't mention what I've said at school."

"I won't," promised Andy. "But I'd think it's something to brag about that your parents were in the Olympics."

"That's just it. Everyone would think I'm bragging—or maybe making it up."

Andy left to go pull Dru off a garden tractor. It was time to meet their mother.

While the two of them were waiting in the warm sunshine near the Buzzard's Roost, Andy thought about all that Marilyn had told him. She acted so aloof to everyone else, and suddenly she was treating him like an old, special friend. Perhaps he was as good a friend as she had; it worried him a bit. Still, it wouldn't hurt him to keep quiet about all she'd said. Anyway, he doubted his classmates would believe the part about her parents being in the Olympics. He wasn't certain that he believed it himself. He'd seen Olympic riding events on television and had been dazzled by them. How could Mr. Peck, who looked so lifeless, have ever done anything dazzling? Andy was thinking about it when Marilyn and her father came out of the store. Marilyn stopped. "Dad, this is Andy from school."

Mr. Peck shook hands without saying anything. Those green eyes looked dead still.

Patting Dru on the shoulder, Marilyn said, "And this is his sister, Dru."

Dru smiled at Mr. Peck but did not speak. He said hello to her, but did not smile.

Marilyn said, "Guess what Dru-for-Drucilla wants for Christmas?"

Mr. Peck said matter-of-factly, "A doll."

"No, a wheelbarrow." Marilyn and Andy laughed, but Mr. Peck remained solemn. Looking at Dru, he said, "Good luck." Then with the least bit more expression, he said, "I'm glad to meet you, Andy. I've heard Marilyn speak of you."

"I saw you in the library once," said Andy. "I like to read the aviation magazines."

Mr. Peck said, "The town has a nice library. We hadn't known what to expect in Georgia."

"Yes, sir," agreed Andy. "Did you see that article in the new *Aviation Week* about—"

Before he could finish the question his mother came

along. "I'm late, and I'm sorry," she said. "Everybody in this county must be shopping today; there were long lines at every cash register. I hope you two have been okay."

"We're fine," said Andy. He looked around to introduce Marilyn and her father, but they had left.

Superdad
and Super Gifts

It was almost Christmas before the poet laureate turned in another poem. Andy saw her put it in Mrs. Todd's mailbox. Next afternoon Mrs. Todd said, "All right, before we settle down to our English lesson, we've a treat: a new contribution from our own poet laureate. "It's 'Superdad,' by Ruby Dubb.

My father is a computer whiz
    But that's only part of what he is.
He's a mathematician, a physicist, too,
    Electronics expert like you never knew.

At tennis, he's a champion; at golf, he's a pro.
    He goes skiing on water; he goes skiing on snow.

He's also a painter, a musician to boot,
    He plays the piano, the guitar, and flute.

He's a pilot, scuba diver, hang glider, playboy,
    Being with him is always a joy.
He loves to throw parties, we have quite a few,
    Next time he throws one, we'll invite all of you."

Andy was confused. Marilyn hadn't wanted him to tell that her father had been a champion horseback rider; it might have been considered bragging. Well, what were these other claims about him? He couldn't imagine much else that she could have dreamed up to include in the poem. Maybe that was it; maybe everything was dreamed up.

Mrs. Todd looked at Marilyn and smiled. "Very nice," she said, putting the poem in the top drawer of her desk. "Now we must settle down to work. With just two more days before the holidays, we've lots to do. Open your books to page 118."

Dave asked, "Aren't we gonna talk about the poem?"

"Why don't we just enjoy Marilyn's poems without criticizing them?" said Mrs. Todd. "Later we'll have some poems in our textbook that we'll discuss, but let's look on our poet laureate's offerings from now on as a bonus, in effect, and just enjoy them."

Andy figured this was because the discussion on the last poem had become too personal, but Marilyn said, "It's all right, Mrs. Todd, I can take criticism."

"Yes, I know you can. But I expect we'd better concentrate now on prepositions. Open your books, please."

The poem may not have been discussed during class period, but it was the talk of the boys and girls after school. The girls were delighted by the prospect of a party at the resort. Andy heard Patsy telling Lena, "Now you and Sue be real nice to her. We don't want to miss out on a big deal." Even the boys thought it would be neat to go to Garden Hills as invited guests and have a chance to look around. Rip told Andy, "Unless those guards decide to chase us out again!"

Blake said, "Oh, they'll let anybody in if they have a reason for being there. My daddy goes up there to talk to them about tractors and things that they've bought from him, and he doesn't have any trouble getting in."

Andy boarded the bus and sat down by Blake, in front of Emily and Karen. Louisa was across the aisle.

Emily said excitedly, "Won't it be fun to go to a party at Garden Hills?"

Karen asked, "How could you have a party without a mother? How will Marilyn do that?"

"Her father'll have it catered," explained Emily. "When you're rich, you hire things done."

"Oh, goodie!" said Karen. "Well, Louisa, you spend that night with me, and my mother'll take us. Emily, you plan to ride with us, too."

Emily said, "Oh, I imagine Marilyn's father will send one of those Garden Hills limousines to pick all of us up."

"With a chauffeur!" squealed Louisa. "How thrilling!"

Andy told them that, from the way they were talking, anyone would suppose they'd already been invited to the resort. The girls insisted that it was only a matter of time till they would be.

Two days later, school let out for the holidays, and Marilyn had not said anything about a party. On the bus going home, Louisa said, "Probably we'll get our invitations in the mail."

"Look," said Andy, "Marilyn didn't say it was gonna happen."

"But she did," insisted Emily. "She said so in a poem."

"Well, she didn't say it would be during the holidays."

"That's right," agreed Karen. "Maybe there's too much going on just now. I'll bet they'll wait and have a Valentine party."

"Oh, won't that be fun!" said Louisa. "Let's get our mothers to make us red-and-white party dresses." Their mothers were good seamstresses. "Maybe we should get them to make Marilyn one, too. I'll bet she'd like that. With her mother being dead and all, she probably doesn't have anybody who makes things for her."

By the time Andy got off the bus, the girls were talking as if there were no doubt about it: the class would be invited to a grand Valentine ball at Garden Hills.

Andy spent the holidays in North Carolina visiting his mother's family. He didn't see any of his classmates till the day school started again. When he got off the bus, he went

over to the bike rack, where Jason was parking the new
BMX he'd gotten for Christmas. There were three new
bikes in the rack, and as Andy and Jason crossed the schoolyard, there were other signs of holiday gifts: bright-colored
caps and scarves that must have been presents, sweaters
and coats that looked as if they were being worn for the
first time, new book satchels and lunch boxes.

Andy's gifts had been fishing equipment. He and his
father liked to fish, and for a long time, he'd wanted a
special rod and reel and a pair of waders. He'd received
them and a tackle box, as well. Of course, it was too cold
to use them now, but it was fun to think about the good
times he'd have with them later.

Across the highway, at the airstrip, there was a bright
red plane. It looked as new and shiny as the big wheelbarrow Santa Claus had brought Dru. "You don't suppose
it was somebody's Christmas present, do you?" asked Andy.

"Could have been," said Jason, studying the twin-
engined plane. "What is it?"

"A Beechcraft Baron."

"Just a little 'stocking stuffer.' " As if Andy didn't know
what he meant, Jason explained, "That's what Mom calls
anything small to help fill up a Christmas stocking."

Tubby Williams came along just then, wearing a fur hat
that was obviously new. Jason kidded him. "With that thing
on, I thought you were a bear coming across the yard!"

"Oh, yeah?" said Tubby. "You'll wish you had one when
it snows." It almost never snowed in the part of Georgia

where Flag City was located. The climate, right for golfing practically year-round, was one reason for Garden Hills being there.

The three boys went together to their room, where early arrivals were chatting excitedly about who got what for Christmas. In addition to clothes and bikes, gifts included cameras, tape recorders, games, candy, and money. Sue had been given a puppy, a Brittany spaniel, that was so cute, according to her, she hated to come to school. Andy knew that it must be special, in that case, because Sue liked school.

Karen said that her main gift had been a cordless phone, which she liked, and Patsy said she'd received an elegant lighted mirror—the kind she'd been wanting.

"Now you can see how beautiful you are!" said Jason.

Patsy didn't realize he was teasing her, but Emily did. She teased him by saying that if he looked into a lighted mirror, it would probably blow a fuse.

Just then Marilyn arrived, and Lena asked her, "What'd Santa Claus bring you?"

"Nothing."

"What?" shouted Lena.

"Well, nothing special," said Marilyn, with a shrug.

Lena said, "I thought anybody who lived at Garden Hills would have had the best Christmas of all. I thought you'd have got more presents than anybody."

Marilyn said, "What you get doesn't show how good a Christmas you had."

"It does to me," said Lena, holding the collar of her new suede jacket closely to her throat.

Jason said, "Santa Claus probably couldn't get past the security guards at Garden Hills!"

"Yeah," agreed Matt. "He probably got turned away 'cause he didn't have on a tie."

Rip, as if he were one of the guards at the resort, said, "No, absolutely not, you can't come in! Garden Hills folks won't go for a pudgy ol' man in a red-and-white suit. And they sure don't want those reindeer messing about on the grounds."

Marilyn laughed, along with everyone else.

After school, Patsy and Andy were crossing the playground at the same time, and Patsy said, "I knew Marilyn wasn't rich."

"Who said she was?"

"She did. At least, she let us believe she was."

"She let you believe anything you wanted to," said Andy.

"Well," said Patsy, huffily, "Lena asked her when we were all going to be invited to that party she wrote about, and all she said was, 'It was a poem.' How do you like that?"

"I like it okay," said Andy, as Patsy turned and headed toward her bus, and he went on to his. But he admitted to himself, and then to his friends on the bus, that Marilyn confused him. "She can be so friendly at times," he said.

"And so distant at others," said Karen. "Anytime any of us acts the least bit chummy, she turns cool and acts like she doesn't really know us—or want to know us—very well."

Louisa said, "Maybe she doesn't want *us* to know *her* any better than we do. Still, I think she'd like to be our friend."

"But friends visit each other," insisted Karen. "Emily and I have asked her to come over. We've even told her that our mothers would take her home, but she never accepts."

Blake asked, "Does she ever invite any of the girls to go home with her?"

Karen said, "That poem about inviting us to one of her father's parties is the closest we've come to an invitation!" Andy didn't tell them that he doubted Marilyn and her father were really among the elite of Garden Hills; Marilyn, after all, was his friend too. "I just don't understand her," concluded Karen.

"Maybe that's because she's a poet," said Louisa. "But really, I wish we could help her. Can you imagine not getting any Christmas presents?"

By mid-January, most of the sixth-graders—the ones who liked Marilyn, as well as those who didn't—felt certain that she was no richer than they were. Patsy, sounding like a very snobbish woman instead of a sixth-grade girl, said, "She may live at Garden Hills, but I don't think she really *belongs* there."

Then Marilyn showed up at school one morning, and

all doubts about her wealth vanished. She was wearing a wrist television set.

"Oh, that's soooo cute!" squealed Louisa. "Why, it's no bigger than a Walkman."

"Wow!" said Cal, crossing the room so that he could see it better. He was followed by Jason, Tubby Williams, and Rip. Soon all the boys and most of the girls had gathered around Marilyn's desk.

Mrs. Todd came into the room, and when the wrist television set had been shown to her, she said, "My goodness! Just look at that!" The set was turned to a morning talk show. The picture was clear and in color, but there was no sound. Mrs. Todd shook her head as if she couldn't believe what she was seeing. "Amazing!" she said. "I didn't know there *was* such a thing."

"I knew there was such a thing," said Cal, "but I didn't know that I knew anybody who could afford one."

"Yeah," said Tubby. "My daddy says one of 'em costs more than a real television."

"It *is* a real television," corrected Marilyn, taking it off her wrist and handing it to Jason so that he could have a closer look.

"I mean more than a big set that you'd put in the house."

"Lots more," agreed Cal, taking the set from Jason. "At least, the good ones do."

Sue said, "Maybe that's not a good one."

"You'd better believe it's a good 'un!" said Cal, pointing

at the manufacturer's name. "It's the best there is." He handed the set to Mrs. Todd.

Andy had seldom seen Mrs. Todd appear so excited; it was as if she were one of the children. "Does it have sound?" she asked.

"Yes, ma'am," said Marilyn. "Turn that little knob there to the right."

Mrs. Todd turned the knob, and the volume came up so loud that she jumped, almost dropping the set. When she'd adjusted the volume, she held the set out so that everyone could watch—when they gathered in close—a science-fiction writer being interviewed.

When she switched off the program, Mrs. Todd said, "Not many years ago *this* might have been considered science fiction."

Patsy asked Marilyn, "Did your father buy it for you?"

"No."

"Then where'd you get it?"

Marilyn looked at her, and Andy half-expected her to say, "I'll reveal it in a poem," but Marilyn said only, "It was given to me."

The Showdown

Dave was the troublemaker, thought Andy. If he'd kept his mouth shut about what his father had said, maybe everything would have gone along the same as usual.

It began before school one morning in February. Early arrivals were talking, and Dave confronted Marilyn as angrily as if he'd caught her taking something that belonged to him. He said, "I saw you at McDonald's last night."

"Yes, I know. I waved at you."

"Was that your father with you? That man in the cowboy hat?"

"Yes."

"I thought it was," said Dave. "And when I told my

father that he was a big, rich man from Garden Hills, Dad just laughed at me. He said, 'I see that guy when we haul gravel up there. He's one of the crew that keeps the grounds.' Then he laughed some more and said, 'Why, he ain't no more a big, rich man than I am. He ain't nothing but a glorified hired hand.' "

Lena joined in: "Why'd you make up all that about what he was?" In a mimicking tone, she added, "I know, *It was a poem*."

"It was about how my father used to be,' said Marilyn, rearranging the books in her desk.

Dave continued to nag her. "And my brother, who was attacked by that big ol' dog up there, said he knows the dog by now and that it don't any more belong to you than the man in the moon. He said it belongs to an old couple who live near you." When Marilyn didn't reply, Dave added, "He delivers their paper, and he ought to know!"

Marilyn looked him in the eye and asked, "Did he tell you that the horse I wrote about is not mine either? He should have. It belongs to the resort. They bought horses when the stables were finished. I get to ride for helping look after them."

Emily reached across and patted Marilyn's hand. "You don't have to explain anything to Dave. It's best to ignore him; that's what we do."

Dave said, "I guess that fine wrist TV's not yours either?"

"It's mine," said Marilyn, and she opened a book and didn't answer any more of his questions.

Although many of the sixth-graders had begun to wonder how Marilyn really fit into the scheme of things at Garden Hills, Andy, along with everyone else, was shocked to hear Marilyn's father described as "a glorified hired hand." Some of the boys and girls looked saddened as well as surprised. Patsy, Sue, and Lena may have looked pleased; Andy wasn't sure.

At recess Andy told Dave, "You've gotta quit pestering Marilyn."

"Oh, yeah?"

"Yeah."

Dave asked loudly, "Who says so?"

"I do," said Andy, louder than he'd meant to. He didn't really want to pick a fight, but somebody had to try to make Dave shut up.

At the sound of raised voices, the other boys gathered around. Dave and Andy were the same size; it should be a good match.

But Rip, who often egged on his friends in scraps, suddenly became a peacemaker. He did a perfect imitation of Mr. Gray: "Young men, we'll have none of this!" Taking Andy by the collar with one hand and Dave by the other, he held them at arm's length. "You will be calm and you will explain to me what has transpired."

It was funny to some of the boys, but Andy was still mad. Rip said, "All right, Andy, you may speak first."

Andy said angrily, "Tell Dave to lay off Marilyn. What business is it of his whether her poems are based on cold facts or not?"

Turning to Dave, Rip asked in his Mr. Gray voice, "Very well, young man, what business is it of yours?"

Rip was so comical that it was hard for Andy to stay mad, but Dave, as always, was dead serious. "Because they're lies," he shouted. "And liars should be punished."

"I can tell we're not going to work this out," said Rip. "You will both report to my office this afternoon, at which time you will write one hundred times, 'Rip Larsen is the greatest.' "

Jason asked, "The greatest what?"

"I'll give it thought," said Rip, doing a consistent job of being Mr. Gray instead of himself. He kept the routine going until the bell rang, when he made Dave and Andy shake hands.

On the way back inside, Rip nudged Andy and whispered, "I forgot to tell you, King Kong, that I wrestled Dave at the Y last Saturday, and he's stronger than he looks. He'd have whipped you good."

Andy said, "Thank you, Mr, Gray," and they both laughed as they settled into their places in line.

Even though they hadn't had to fight it out, Andy felt certain that Dave would leave Marilyn alone now. But Dave was not put off. At the beginning of English he said, "Mrs. Todd, our poet laureate's been telling lies."

"What do you mean, Dave?"

"Well, those poems about all those pets and things, the big dog and her horse, and all that. Well, they're not true. She doesn't own all those things."

Marilyn said, "I never said the poems were true."

"Why, you did," insisted Dave. "You said you had that . . . that . . . er . . . menagerie . . . in the very first poem."

"No, I wrote about a menagerie, but the only thing I said when we talked about it was that I'd never had a dog, which is true. I've been careful not to tell a lie when we were just talking. It's not my fault that everybody believed the poems."

Dave said, "Mrs. Todd, when we were writing poems for the newspaper contest, you told us to write about something that was true. And she didn't!"

Mrs. Todd said firmly, "No, Dave, you have that wrong. When some of you were having trouble thinking of what to write about, I said that you *could,* or that you *might,* write about something that had happened to you. I certainly never said anyone *had to.*" When Dave looked disgruntled still, she added, "And Marilyn produced a poem we all enjoyed, didn't she? If it wasn't true, then it was a flight of fancy that she shared with all of us."

Sue said, "But Mrs. Todd, some of the things that Marilyn wrote were true, or partly true, and part of them weren't. Like that St. Bernard puppy. Some of the boys had seen it up at Garden Hills, so naturally we thought all the rest of the poem was true, too. That doesn't seem right."

Marilyn said, "It's called *poetic license.* The poet takes liberty with facts in order to achieve a desired effect." Andy couldn't help thinking that she sounded almost like Sue, giving a memorized definition of something.

"Very good!" said Mrs. Todd. "And Sue, can't you see that the desired effects in the poems have been highly entertaining?" She smiled, but Sue did not. "And, too, sometimes a poet writes about life as he or she thinks it should be instead of exactly the way it is."

Andy thought, That's what Marilyn's been doing, just as Marilyn said, "Yes, ma'am, maybe I was telling how I wish things were." She paused and added, "But I'm sorry if I did wrong."

Jason said, "You didn't do anything wrong. Write us another poem!"

"I may have misled you," said Marilyn—almost as if she were talking to herself. "Even though I didn't lie outright, I knew everyone thought I really had all those things." Then she brightened: "And it was fun to hear everybody laugh when one of my poems was read. It made me feel good."

"Still," said Sue, "you deceived us."

"That's enough, Sue," said Mrs. Todd in a tone that meant everyone should drop the subject, but Marilyn continued as if she hadn't understood. "For a little while, I'd imagine that what I'd written was true. Like I could imagine how much fun it would be to have two sisters and a baby brother."

"Yeah," snarled Lena. "Who were they?"

"Didn't you hear me?" snapped Mrs. Todd, looking at Lena.

Again, Marilyn continued: "They belong to Charley Berry,

my father's good friend. He's my good friend, too. He gave me the wrist television." She spoke softly still and with no expression. Andy was reminded of a hypnosis demonstration that had been on television.

Mrs. Todd looked more worried than Andy had ever seen her. Maybe she thought Marilyn was in a trance.

Marilyn went on: "He said I'd earned the television set for all the babysitting I've done when his family's in Georgia. But I wasn't expecting a reward."

Mrs. Todd went back and patted Marilyn on the shoulders. "That's enough, dear," she said softly. "We need to get back to our lesson."

When they were leaving the building after the final bell, Andy hurried to catch up with Marilyn. "Slow down!" he said when he was even with her. "There's something I want to ask you."

Patsy and Sue came up back of them. In a loud voice so she'd be certain to be heard, Patsy said, "My father's a millionaire. We're going to have a grand party. Could you come?"

"Oh, yes," squealed Sue, in an affected tone, "I can come. Will you send one of your limousines to fetch me?"

"Why, yes, of course," said Patsy. "I'll send a limousine. Oh, no, I'm sorry, I forgot: My father's not a millionaire; he's a glorified hired hand!"

They walked away in the direction of their bus, laughing

hysterically and calling loudly, "Glorified hired hand! Glorified hired hand!"

By then Andy and Marilyn were almost to the El Camino where Marilyn's father was waiting. Andy was afraid Mr. Peck might have heard Patsy and Sue yelling "Glorified hired hand." Of course, he wouldn't have known they were talking about him.

"What did you want to ask me?" asked Marilyn calmly as if she hadn't even heard Patsy and Sue.

"I was wondering if you'd like help with our math for tomorrow. I'll be at the library downtown in about an hour."

"Thank you," said Marilyn, "but I don't go to the library now. My father doesn't feel like bringing me."

A New Season

During the final weeks of winter, it seemed to Andy that Marilyn stayed to herself more than ever. Sometimes she'd chat with other girls on the playground, and a few times she had talked with him and Jason. But mostly she stood out near the edge of the schoolyard by herself, looking as somber as the late winter skies. Sometimes she didn't go outside at all and would sit at her desk, leafing through books or staring into space until the others returned to class.

Eventually there were signs of spring: the countryside was turning green, softball season got under way, and—to Andy's special delight—traffic picked up at the airstrip of

Garden Hills. "Warmer weather's bringing out more golf-ers," said Jason, as they looked at the three planes that had landed during recess.

But March, as always, was unpredictable, and there was a drastic change by the following day. It was drizzly and cold. Most of their classmates stayed indoors during recess, but Andy and Jason went onto the playground. They were hoping for a better look at a Cessna Citation that was set for takeoff at the airstrip.

Andy was surprised to find Marilyn outside. She stood at the edge of the playground where the boys usually gath-ered. "While no one was around," she explained, "I came to see what it's like over here." Looking out toward the airstrip, she said, "It's not very pretty—a highway and a runway. I like my tree better." She motioned toward the big oak in the far corner of the playground.

"The tree shuts out your view," said Jason

"But it's nicer than the view it shuts out," insisted Mar-ilyn.

Jason laughed. "All right, you win!"

Marilyn started away just as Dave came out. He said angrily, "Girls are not supposed to be over here."

Marilyn turned to face him, but before she could say anything, Jason said, "There's no rule against it."

"I don't care," said Dave. "It's an unwritten law."

"Unwritten law!" said Jason. "My gosh!"

"That's swearing," said Dave. "*My gosh* stands for *my God*. You'll go to hell."

"Not today!" said Jason, walking off. Andy would have followed him, but Marilyn had come back to where they were standing, and he didn't want to leave her alone with Dave. She asked Dave, "Do you really think Jason will suffer because he said *my gosh?*"

"I know he will," said Dave. "It's in the Bible."

Marilyn said, "But *the Lord is just in all his ways, and kind in all his doings.*" She was quoting from one of the Psalms. Andy remembered someone reciting it at a youth fellowship program in his church. "I read the Bible too," continued Marilyn. "There's some great poetry in it."

"No, there's not," said Dave. "The Bible is God's word. It's not poetry." He turned and headed back toward the building in a huff. The bell rang a moment later, and Andy and Marilyn went back inside, too.

It was time for math lesson, but Dave said, "Mrs. Todd, Marilyn says there's poems in the Bible. Tell her there ain't."

"Why, no, Dave. Instead of telling her *there aren't,* why don't I tell you there are. But we must concentrate on our math now. We'll get back to poetry this afternoon." It wasn't easy to keep Mrs. Todd away from a lesson.

By noon the drizzle had turned to steady rain and no one was permitted to go outside. Mrs. Todd arranged for her students to have extra time in the library after they'd returned from the cafeteria. Or they could stay in the room. Andy stayed in the room; he needed to work on his English assignment. While he was rewriting it, he overheard a conversation between Marilyn and Mrs. Todd. Marilyn had started to the library, but Mrs. Todd had spoken to her. "We've missed your poems," she said. "Isn't it time you wrote another one? After all, you're our poet laureate."

Marilyn said, "Maybe the class should elect another poet laureate."

"Why, no, dear, I didn't mean it in that way. I just thought you might write something else for us."

"I haven't been able to think of anything that the class might like," said Marilyn.

"If you don't want to write a humorous poem," said Mrs. Todd, "write a serious one. Poets produce poetry, no matter what's happening around them. Anyway, we miss your contributions." She smiled at Marilyn, who went ahead to the library.

At the beginning of English, Mrs. Todd said, "I'd planned to read you a few poems about the arrival of spring. The subject has inspired poets over the ages. But today is so unlike spring, perhaps I should leave them till another time."

"Oh, don't," said Louisa. "It'll make us feel better to hear about the way it's supposed to be."

Mrs. Todd looked pleased. "Very well," she said, and she opened a book and read three poems to the class. Andy didn't care much for the first two, but he liked the third. It began, "I wandered lonely as a cloud . . ."

Mrs. Todd put away the book and said, "One of my other favorites about the coming of spring is in the Bible."

Looking at Dave, she added, "There's a great deal of poetry in the Bible. The passage I'm recalling is in the *Song of Solomon*. It's about winter being past and flowers starting to bloom. It mentions that a time of singing has come, which I think is nice. Then it says, 'And the voice of the turtle is heard in our land.' "

"Turtle?" said Blake.

"It's really the turtledove," said Mrs. Todd, taking up her textbook. "And now it's time to get back to our lesson on compound subjects and compound predicates."

When several of the students groaned, she said, "Cheer up! We'll start something new tomorrow."

On Thursday, Marilyn dropped a poem into Mrs. Todd's mailbox. Her friends looked forward to hearing it the next afternoon.

All day Friday, it seemed to Andy that Marilyn looked stronger than she had in recent weeks. He guessed Mrs. Todd had known that writing a poem would make her feel better somehow. That wasn't easy for him to understand— writing anything was just about the last thing that would help his feelings.

At the beginning of English, Mrs. Todd said, "Before we start our lesson, we have a new poem from our poet laureate. It's called 'Looking Up.' "

Good, thought Andy, that's a cheerful-sounding title. It'll be a funny one.

"And, of course, the poem is by Ruby Dubb," said Mrs. Todd. Then she read:

We used to go outside at night,
    my mother and father and I
We'd look at the constellations
    and other wonders in the sky.
Then we'd go inside again,
    and before we said goodnight,
We'd have delicious refreshments,
    things my mother called "light."

My father no longer looks up at the sky,
    now that my mother is dead
And he doesn't have light refreshments,
    he drinks beer and whisky instead.
It helps him forget his sorrow,
    so he drinks everything he can find.
Instead of losing his sorrow,
    some say he's losing his mind.

There are days when I think he's better;
    his best friend says he'd bet every cent
That soon he'll be able to cope once more
    with the computer business he helped invent.
I miss the way he used to be;
    surely he'll be well by and by,
Yet sometimes I go outside at night
    to be certain that stars are still in the sky.

On the bus going home, Andy and Blake talked about the poem with the girls across the aisle. "I couldn't believe it," said Karen. "All her other poems have been funny, or at least happy ones, and today's was *so* sad. I could've cried!" She added quickly, "Oh, I'm sorry, Louisa, I wasn't thinking. I wasn't talking about you."

Usually, whenever Mrs. Todd finished reading a poem to the class—any poem, not just Marilyn's—Louisa would squeal and declare it cute. A few times she had said something was sad, but always she was among the first to respond to a poem. This time she had burst out crying.

"I don't know what came over me," said Louisa. "But I'm all right now."

Karen said, "Mrs. Todd said you *felt* the poem. That's nothing to be ashamed of."

"Maybe the poem wasn't true," said Emily. "After all, none of Marilyn's others have been true—at least, not *all* true."

"Yeah," agreed Karen. "Maybe it was poetic license."

Louisa said, "I've forgotten what *poetic license* means."

"It means when somebody writing something gets away from the real truth and comes up with something else."

"For the desired effect," said Andy, remembering Marilyn's definition of it. He didn't tell them that the poem was probably the only one Marilyn had written that was all true. He suspected the girls knew it, anyway, but just didn't want to believe it quite yet.

"Right!" said Karen. "And in Marilyn's poem, the desired effect was to make it sad."

"It was sad, for sure," said Louisa, brightening a bit. "I'm just glad it was *poetic license*."

Royal Court at Recess

Andy's father took Andy and Rip with him to the boat show in Macon. Jason was to have gone, too, but he had a sore throat and his mother kept him home. Matt, Blake, and Cal had gone the night before. People in Flag City were interested in boats because of the big lakes that had been built along the Chattahoochee and other rivers in Georgia. Mr. Haley had said that maybe next year he and Andy would buy a boat.

Andy, his father, and Rip had a good time looking at boats on display, but Mr. Haley tired of the show before the boys did. He sat down in the refreshment area to wait while they took in a few more exhibits.

Andy noticed that when his father had been with them, the attendants at the booths were especially nice. But evidently two boys by themselves didn't look like prospective customers, because they were watched carefully and reminded frequently to look at the equipment but not touch it. That could have been because Rip was inclined to handle everything.

They were hurrying to see as much as they could, and when they rounded the corner of one of the exhibits they almost collided with a man who was hurrying in the opposite direction. Andy was set for a "Watch-where-you're-going" remark called back to them, but the man stopped and said, "Oh, excuse me. I was in too big a hurry to catch up with my friends." Just as Andy realized it was Charley Berry, Mr. Berry recognized him and Rip. "Why, I know you boys!" he said heartily. "How's it going? Are you enjoying the show?"

"Yes, sir," said Andy, but Rip added, "The automobile show was better."

Mr. Berry laughed. As he started away, he said, "Try an air show. They're best of all."

"Yes, sir, we will," said Andy. He looked to see who Mr. Berry was joining and saw Marilyn's father standing in the aisle a short distance away. At the same time, Rip said, "Look! There's Marilyn!"

"Yeah," said Andy. "That's her father next to her."

Mr. Berry put one arm around Marilyn and propped the other one on her father's shoulder, and the three of them walked away. "I'll quit worrying about her,"said Rip, "if they pal around with Mr. Berry."

Rip, along with many of Andy's friends, had been concerned about Marilyn since her last poem had been read in class. Louisa especially had been worried. She'd told Andy that they must do something.

The following afternoon, Louisa talked to Andy again. "My mother said she'd make a costume for Marilyn to wear to the party." Mrs. Todd had announced that in a few weeks, sixth-graders were to come to school dressed as their favorite characters from books. "But I don't know if Marilyn will come over to let my mom take measurements and all. She could come home with us on the bus if we got permission ahead. Do you think her father would pick her up afterward?"

"My mother'll take her home," said Andy. "I'm sure she wouldn't mind."

"Well, what about going with me tomorrow to ask her?"

"Oh, I'll ask her tonight."

"No, I mean Marilyn. Maybe if you'd go with me at recess to talk with her, she'd accept." Before Andy could answer, Louisa added, "She trusts you," as if Marilyn didn't really trust anyone else in the class.

"I'll go," said Andy, and the following day at recess, he and Louisa headed across the schoolyard. It was a nice day and, as usual, most of the boys had gathered at the edge of the playground. Girls were in a different part of the yard, the side that was sunny in the morning. Marilyn was alone at the end of the playground that was shaded by the big oak.

Jason called, "Hey, King Kong, come on! There's a jet Commander on the runway."

"I'll see you later," yelled Andy. "Tell the Commander to wait!" He hurried to catch up with Louisa.

Marilyn seemed surprised that anyone else had come out to the big oak. She was studying a plant that grew near its trunk.

"Mind if we join you?" asked Andy.

"No, I don't mind." She leaned over and touched the plant. "I love ferns, don't you?" Smiling at him, she added, "There were such pretty ones in California."

"We wanted to talk to you," said Louisa. "You know the costume day that Mrs. Todd's planning?" Although there was no one else within hearing distance, she lowered her voice as if she were telling a secret: "Emily and Karen and I plan to come as the *Little Women*."

Marilyn said quickly, "But there are four *Little Women*."

"That's just it. We need you to be one."

"Thank you, but I don't think so." She looked at Andy. "Who're you going to be?"

Andy said, "Not one of the little women." Louisa giggled, and Marilyn smiled.

"My mother'll make a costume for you if you'll come and be fitted for it. Would you do that?"

Andy said, "Mom will take you home afterward."

When Marilyn looked surprised, Louisa explained, "That's

'cause my mother doesn't drive, but Andy's does. Anyway, we've worked it out. Will you help us?" In an almost pleading tone, she added, "You can be whichever one of the Little Women you choose. You'll have first choice. Will you do it?"

"I'll have to see," said Marilyn just as Patsy, Sue, and Lena started toward them. Andy had never seen them speak to Marilyn on the playground, and he knew they were coming now out of curiosity.

Louisa asked again, "Will you do it?"

"I'll have to see," said Marilyn. "But thank you. I thank both of you for . . ."

She was interrupted by Patsy loudly saying to Andy and Louisa, "Well, well! I thought this was Miss Garden Hills' private corner of the playground. You mean she lets you visit her?"

Sue said, "Maybe this is the royal court. Is Her Highness receiving guests, or do we have to have appointments?"

Lena said, "We must be careful. Her Highness might have us beheaded if we don't behave to suit her."

"Yeah," said Patsy. "Bow down and kiss her feet."

Lena, as always, was happy to do anything Patsy suggested. She knelt down and leaned over as if she were kissing the ground near Marilyn's feet. Andy almost wished Marilyn would kick her, but Marilyn turned and walked away.

"That was ugly," said Louisa. She turned and followed Marilyn across the yard.

"Well, lah-dee-dah!" said Patsy, swishing her hips in an exaggerated manner as she and Sue, followed by Lena, walked away.

The bell rang then, and everyone started back inside. Jason, on one side of Andy, said, "The Commander's still there. Do you suppose it'll take off before lunch?" and Louisa, on the other side, whispered, "I believe Marilyn'll accept our invitation, don't you?"

Andy shrugged. "Who knows?" The answer would do for both questions.

The Ride
to Garden Hills

Often the next week, Andy saw Louisa or Emily or Karen—
sometimes all three—talking with Marilyn at recess, and
on Friday Marilyn went home with them on the bus. The
girls got off two blocks before Andy did, and he assured
them that his mother had remembered the date and
would be at Louisa's house at five-thirty to take Marilyn
home.

"If you've finished your homework, you can ride with
us," said Mrs. Haley when it was time to go.

"It's finished," said Andy, closing his social-studies book.
"Ask me anything you want to know about Spain and Por-
tugal."

"We must go there someday," said Mrs. Haley. "Let's save our money."

Andy got into the back seat, so Marilyn could sit up front with his mother.

When they got to Louisa's house, she came out to the car with Marilyn. "Wouldn't you like to ride with us?" asked Mrs. Haley.

"Thank you," said Louisa. "But I'm cooking supper so Mama can keep working on the costumes."

Mrs. Haley teased her: "In that case, we may just stop back by and eat with you!" By then, Marilyn was in the car and they drove away.

"Lou's a marvelous seamstress," said Mrs. Haley. She was talking about Louisa's mother.

"Yes, she is," agreed Marilyn.

"I can't wait to see the dresses. I was with her when she picked out the material. Which color's to be yours?"

"The pink."

"Wonderful!" said Mrs. Haley. "I just love dainty prints in soft colors."

"Me too," said Marilyn, which Andy thought was a bit strange, considering she'd never worn anything but dark, solid colors—except the time she was having her picture made. Marilyn asked, "Did you know we're to have bonnets, too?"

"I did indeed! Lou showed me the pattern. I told her that I wished she'd make me one of those!" She and Marilyn laughed, and they talked more about the costumes,

Mrs. Haley doing most of the talking, till they stopped for Dru.

Dru had been playing at a friend's house. "I'll run in and get her," said Andy, starting from the car, but his mother said she'd go. She needed to talk to the other child's mother about the kindergarten car pool.

Alone with Marilyn, Andy couldn't think of anything to say. It was the first chance they'd had for a private conversation in a long time. Marilyn was quiet, too. Finally, Andy said, "Some really neat books have been put on the 'What's New?' table at the library downtown. I saw two big poetry ones yesterday. You oughta start coming back down there."

"Maybe I should," said Marilyn.

"If your father doesn't feel like bringing you, my mother could pick you up sometimes when we're going."

"Thank you, but I wouldn't want to put her to so much trouble."

"Oh, she wouldn't mind."

"Besides," said Marilyn, "my father's better. Maybe he'll bring me. The reason we haven't been lately is that he's been real busy. His crew's reseeding one of the golf courses."

"I'm glad he's better," said Andy.

"Oh, me too!" said Marilyn. "He's more like he was before Mama died. He's *lots* better." She said it with such conviction that Andy wasn't certain whether she meant to convince him or herself that it was so.

His mother and Dru arrived at the car then, and they

went directly to Garden Hills. At the main entrance, Mrs. Haley asked, "Will the guard let us in?"

"I'll tell him it's okay," said Marilyn. But when the guard saw that she was in the car, she didn't have to say anything. He signaled for them to enter.

All the houses for permanent residents were built of wood and had been stained to give them a weathered look. Set well back from the road among tall loblolly pines, they blended into their surroundings, even the big three-storied ones. Marilyn and her father lived in a single-story house at the end of a street that was lined with dogwood trees.

"What a lovely setting," said Mrs. Haley, starting up the long driveway. "A blue lake out front and the green golf course in back. If I lived here, I'd be too busy looking out the window to ever get my housework done!"

"I like to look out the window, too," said Marilyn. "Sometimes I imagine that I'm seeing California trees and that the lake is really an inlet of the Pacific Ocean and that if I walk down to it, I'll see brown pelicans and rocks with seals on them and things like that."

"What a good imagination!" said Mrs. Haley. "I can almost feel a breeze off the ocean!" She and Marilyn laughed together.

When she was getting out of the car, Marilyn thanked Mrs. Haley for the ride home. Then, almost as an after-thought, she asked, "Would you like to come in?"

Dru said, "Yes, we'll come in," and Andy wished his mother would agree to it.

"No, thank you, dear," said Mrs. Haley. "Perhaps some other time."

They had started back down the drive before Mrs. Haley saw that another vehicle was coming up it. Andy recognized the El Camino. "That's Mr. Peck," he said, "Marilyn's father."

Mr. Peck drove the pickup off to the side to make room for them. Dru waved at him as vigorously as if she were trying to flag down a train. Mr. Peck smiled at her and waved back. He winked at Andy as they drew even with him and tipped his cowboy hat to Mrs. Haley.

Marilyn's right, thought Andy. He's better. He's definitely better.

The Last Poem

"Those outfits are marvelous!" said Mrs. Todd. She was looking at Emily, Karen, Louisa, and Marilyn. Today they were the four March sisters of *Little Women*.

Mrs. Todd wore a black dress and a black pointed hat with a wide brim. She was the Wicked Witch of the West from *The Wizard of Oz*. She teased her students: "You've known all the time that I was a witch, haven't you?"

Jason had come as Darth Vader, and Rip as Luke Skywalker, from *Star Wars*. Mrs. Todd wasn't sure that it was good to have characters from a book that had come about because of a movie, but she agreed that their costumes were interesting.

Tubby came as Wilbur from *Charlotte's Web* and refused to say anything but "Oink, oink," all day. Patsy, to no one's surprise, came as Beauty of *Beauty and the Beast.* She'd talked Lena into coming as the beast.

Andy and Blake were characters from biographies they'd been reading of World War II heroes. They wore their camouflage suits, along with garrison caps that Andy's mother had found for them at a yard sale. Andy, wearing dark glasses, became General MacArthur, and Blake, who'd borrowed one of his cousin's bullterriers, pretended to be General Patton.

Mrs. Todd felt that he shouldn't have brought the dog to school, but Blake said it was part of his costume. Without the bullterrier, he insisted, General Patton would have looked like just another general.

During the day there was teasing—most of it good-natured—about the costumes. Occasionally Mrs. Todd had to scold someone, especially when the boys began telling Lena that she should wear her beast costume every day, that it made her look better than usual.

The students were asked to tell a bit about the book from which their character had been taken. When the four Little Women had their turn, they introduced themselves: Karen was Meg, Louisa was Jo, Marilyn was Beth, and Emily was Amy. Dave said, "I've forgotten which one was Beth."

"I am," said Marilyn.

"I mean in the story."

Marilyn said, "The one who died."

"But you don't look sick," said Jason, and everyone, including Marilyn, laughed. She not only didn't look sick, thought Andy, she looked really nice. The pink dress that Louisa's mother had made was especially pretty, and the white pinafore and bonnet added just the right touch.

Everything went well till Tubby said, "Oink, oink," once too often to General Patton's bullterrier, and the dog bit him. It was only a nick on the ankle, but Mrs. Todd sent Tubby to the clinic and Blake home with the dog. The students settled back to their regular lessons.

Afterward Marilyn began wearing brighter-colored clothes to school. Maybe this was because spring somehow called for cheerful colors, but Andy wondered if the costume Louisa's mother had made for her had somehow sparked the idea in Marilyn—or perhaps her father—that her outfits should be brighter. Along with her clothing, her mood, too, seemed sunnier. Although she still kept to herself part of the time, she did not appear as solemn now.

One afternoon, after a visit to Rip's, Andy was riding his bike on the road alongside Garden Hills. Because he'd stayed longer at Rip's than usual, he was hurrying home. He didn't slow down at the spot near the lake to see if Marilyn might be there, but when he was just past it, he heard someone calling to him. He looked back and saw Marilyn, on horseback, coming along the trail nearest the road. There was someone riding another horse, the bay, and Andy felt certain it was the rider with the English accent who'd dismissed him so briskly with, "Excuse us, young man," the other time. Andy waved, but did not stop until Marilyn called, "Wait there!"

He rode his bike onto the shoulder of the road and waited, and when they were nearer, he saw that the man was not the one he remembered. This one looked a bit familiar, but it wasn't until Marilyn had said, "You've met my father," that he realized who it was. It seemed almost funny to him that the only time he'd seen her father without his cowboy hat, he was riding a horse! His hair was brownish-blond and curly, and he was tanned and handsome.

Mr. Peck said, "Hello, Andy. I'm glad to see you again."

"I'm glad to see you, too," said Andy.

"Will you come for a ride with us? There's an extra horse in the stables that we can bring out for you."

Andy looked up at the tall fence with the strands of barbed wire across the top, and Mr. Peck laughed. "Oh, I didn't mean for you to climb the fence! We'll come along to the gate and let you in."

"Thank you," said Andy, "but I'd better not. It's a long way home." He added, "And my mother worries if I'm not there before the sun goes down," sounding as if his mother's concern was an aggravation.

Marilyn's father smiled at him and said, "You're lucky to have your mother. Is your dad at home, too?"

"Yes, but he's not as bad a worrier as Mom is."

Mr. Peck laughed again. His green eyes sparkled in a way that Andy wouldn't have thought possible that day in the library, months ago, when he hadn't known that the sad-faced man was Marilyn's father. "Marilyn has only me," said Mr. Peck. Then he added, "Sorry you can't ride with us."

"I am, too," said Marilyn. Her horse was getting fidgety, and she turned it around and started away. Her father followed her.

"Thank you, anyway," called Andy. He watched as they rode off toward the stables. Marilyn kept to the open, but her father had his horse jump a series of hurdles that had been placed there. He sailed over them as smoothly and as swiftly as if his horse had had wings—and a jet engine. Maybe he *had* ridden in the Olympics, thought Andy as he hurried away.

At recess the next day, he went out to the big oak. "I enjoyed seeing your dad yesterday," he said.

"He enjoyed seeing you, too," said Marilyn.

"He could really ride that horse!"

"Yes, I know," said Marilyn. There was a twinkle in her eyes as if she knew Andy had doubted that her father was all she'd claimed. "But best of all, he's happy again."

"Maybe he's well."

"Charley Berry thinks he is," said Marilyn just as Louisa and Emily arrived. Before Marilyn turned to them she added, "I'll bet the doctors on the Coast will think so, too." She always spoke of "the Coast" as if it were down the street a few blocks instead of in California, two thousand miles away.

Andy went in search of Rip and Jason. Partway across the playground, he met Karen. She had become interested in planes recently and sometimes went out to the boys' gathering place for a better view of them. At the same time, Jason had become interested in Karen; he'd dared Dave to even mention that girls might not be welcome there.

Karen pointed toward the airstrip. "There's nothing on the runway," she said.

"But you never know," said Andy, "when something new will show up."

On Friday, when the final bell rang, Andy remembered a copy of *Sports Illustrated* that he'd borrowed from Rip. He sat back down at his desk to look for it, and by the time he stood up again, everyone was out of the room except Marilyn. She was waiting near Mrs. Todd's desk, although Mrs. Todd was outside.

He looked out the window at the cars alongside the curb and saw that a Garden Hills limousine waited where the El Camino usually parked. Pointing at it, he asked, "Is the limo for you?" Marilyn had told him once that she'd been embarrassed the few times her father had sent a chauffeured car for her. Maybe that's why she was hanging back now; she'd let Patsy and the others catch their bus before she went outside.

"Dad and Charley Berry are waiting for me at the airfield," she said. "I could have walked, but they wanted to make certain I got there on time."

Andy looked at the folded piece of paper that she was holding. "Another poem?" he asked.

"Yes."

"Good! Mrs. Todd'll read it to us Monday."

Marilyn handed him the paper. "It's for you," she said. "If you'd like, you can leave it for Mrs. Todd and the rest of the class. But it's for you."

Andy didn't know what to say. He stammered. "Well, thanks . . . I reckon. I mean, yeah, thanks. I've never had a poem written for me."

"You're welcome . . . I reckon," said Marilyn, and they both laughed. " 'Bye, Andy," she said, and she turned and hurried from the room while he unfolded the sheet of paper.

"See you," he called to her, and then he read the poem:

I've gone to California on the Yellow Daisy plane,
    And I'll live in California by the ocean.
The Pacific will border my happy domain,
    And I'll swim there when I take a notion.

My father will work in the Silicon Valley
    Near a silicon garden and fountain.
He'll get back to computers; I know he won't dally,
    Soon he'll be King of the Silicon Mountain.

We'll live in a house that is out from the city,
    With June-bug and Lori and Anna Marie,
And their mother and father, two dogs and a kitty.
    They'll all be our family; how lucky are we!

I'll keep writing poetry, this much I'm announcing:
    I'll stuff verses in bottles and send them to sea.
If you come across one that's bobbing and bouncing
    You'll find there's a poem, a message from me.

You'll know that I miss you, no doubt you'll suspect
    That I'm still wearing pencils down to the nub,
And maybe you'll smile then when you recollect
    Your poet laureate, Marilyn, who was called
    Ruby Dubb.

When he'd finished reading it, Andy stared at the poem for a long time. Finally, he folded it and dropped it into the box on the corner of Mrs. Todd's desk. Then he started away.

Partway down the hall, he turned and went back to the room. He picked up the poem and put it in his shirt pocket. Monday he could share it with the class.

In the schoolyard, all of the buses had left—and most of the cars. The limousine was almost at the entrance to the Garden Hills airport by now. And just beyond the high fence, on the runway, the Yellow Daisy was set for takeoff.

About the Author

Although he has lived in big cities—Tokyo, New York, London—Robert Burch is most at home in his native Fayette County, Georgia. Like Flag City in *King Kong and Other Poets,* the area has changed from dirt-poor farming country—the setting for some of his earlier books, including *Queenie Peavy*—into an affluent modern community. Cotton fields have given way to shopping centers, airstrips, and golf courses.

Marilyn, in *King Kong and Other Poets,* moves to a small town in Georgia from Saratoga, California (Mr. Burch says, "I once lived there, too!"). He explains that he wanted to write a story about someone who doesn't fit in. "Marilyn doesn't bother at first to try to conform, but then she begins to enjoy acceptance—without correcting the misconceptions that led to it. I enjoyed working with themes of special meaning to me: reality and dreams, indirect and intentional deception, poverty and wealth, and the age-old questions of 'Will I be accepted?' and 'Who am I?' "